A PATIENT ON ATALAYA

or Elena and the First
Time Travel in History

An original screenplay by
DIEGO COSTA MELGAR

A Patient on Atalaya or Elena and the First Time Travel in History

Copyright © Diego Costa Melgar

All rights reserved. Any form of total or partial reproduction, distribution, public communication or transformation of this work in any form, whether electronic, mechanical, photocopying, recording or otherwise, may only be carried out with the prior written permission of the author.

To contact the author, write to **dcosta@dcm.cl**

ISBN: 978-956-420-471-0
Intellectual Property Registry Safe Creative: 2406108213270

First Spanish Paperback Edition: November 2023
First English Paperback Edition: March 2025

Edited by: Daniela Ramírez Pedreros
Prologue by: Victor Soto Martínez
Cover & Interior Design by: María Paz Carvajal Becerra
Translated by: María Paz Carvajal Becerra
Reviewed by: Antonia Palacios Cousiño

Proudly created in Stgo. Chile.

Note:

When reading this script, we recommend that you start with a blank and open mind, so that you have space to imagine the scenes described visually. To situate yourself in each scene, indicated by the numbers located to the right and left of each one, it is necessary to read their headings and descriptions in detail.

Some concepts to keep in mind:

Int. - Scene set inside a building, house, studio, etc.

Ext. - Scene developed outdoors, street, countryside, etc.

O.S. - Off screen, you cannot see the character talking.

Cut to black - literally a sharp cut from the image to black.

Fade out - the image slowly fades to black.

To my family then, now and always.
With all the gratitude, respect and
deep love that they deserve.

```
Prologue to A Patient on Atalaya or Elena and the First
Time Travel in History
```

The Invisible Movies

One

A woman is invited to a TV show. The host, accustomed to dealing with crazy people eager for the spotlight – it is a tabloid show after all – doesn't give much importance to what the woman is saying. But, little by little, her words impact the audience (and they throw him off, force him out of character). The woman has promised the impossible, the outrageous: time travel. More so: to execute a journey through time on live television, in front of everyone. There is no duplicity or deception.

Another important thing: all of this has already happened. What we see is an archival footage, a show from the 1990s, seemingly forgotten. At this point I hope I have captured, to quote Leonardo Di Caprio, not only your *curiosity* but also your *attention*.

Through most of the story, we see the woman trying to convince the man of the truth in her words. But most of all, she tries to challenge the man to break out of his skepticism. Apparently, there is a message that she wants to deliver personally to him and, *also to the rest of the world*, a message that is, according to her, of absolute vital necessity. The doubt is soon transferred to the viewer/reader of the story. Is what she says true? We hope that this will be the case, even if it is unlikely. However, we will soon be left with something else: the mystery of a *why*. The story – like all good stories – begins in surprise and ends in mystery.

If this were a movie, we'd be seeing the opening credits now.

Two

I have told you the anecdote, but we haven't gotten to the heart of the matter yet. I will now address it without further ado. Why read the script of a movie that hasn't been filmed yet? What is this experiment? Is the reader's patience being abused?

Our answer is bound to be ambiguous. Yes and no. Yes, this is an experiment that asks the reader not only for their patience, but also, in a way, for a leap of faith. But, at the same time, we want to make it clear that there are many valid reasons to read cinema, to also see in it - even if it sounds scandalous - a literary form.

The screenplay, as we know it, began its steps as a support for filmmakers, and then – at the hand of Thomas Harper Ince, a producer from the beginning of the 20th century – as a part of the assembly line of film production. In this way, it began to be required to detail information about the interior and exterior scenarios to be filmed, as well as an exact count of the people that would participate in said scenes. Therefore, although it began as a guide, it gradually became a set of instructions, and later a literary form that wanted to be like its severe mother, dramaturgy.

Great writers have lent their services to production companies, such as Scott Fitzgerald and Faulkner, but many times the script was seen either as food, or as a transitory pastime, a sparring partner before these writers faced their real opponents, the novel or the short story. However, the list of writers-screenwriters and writer-cinephiles is very long. Even Borges and Bioy Casares fell into vice (the "seventh vice", as a distinguished cinephile of our lands would say). The Chilean María Luisa Bombal would also do the same with the Argentinian film *The House of Memory* (and was about to sell *The House of Mist* to Hollywood, an English version of her novel). The adaptation of a short story or a novel to the language of cinema was then – and I would dare say that it still is, despite all the water that has passed under the bridge – the wet dream of every writer, and more than once the rights to a text have been granted on the condition of getting their hands on the script.

On the other hand, it would be unfair not to refer here to the great writers of cinema, who throughout the 20th century were carving out the form of the script until they gave it a literary aspect. How can we not think of a Dalton Trumbo (*Spartacus*), made invisible by the anti-communist persecution of the Cold War, or a Fred Nugent, the writer behind *The Searchers*, John Ford's unforgettable film? Do you think *The Empire Strikes Back* is the best movie in the Star Wars saga? Well, much of its complex structure has to do with Leigh Brackett, a writer famous for having corrected the script of *The Big Sleep* by William Faulkner himself. Nowadays, no one could doubt the virtues of Aaron Sorkin (*The Social Network*), who imprints his characteristic verbose style on all of the scripts he writes, or what the revolutionary career of Charlie Kaufman (*Eternal Sunshine of the Spotless Mind*) has meant – especially in terms of form. The latter is important. The script, a form that was originally intended to be adjective, instrumental, has become, in itself, a space for stylistic innovation. Let's think of Tarantino and his stories in media res, his permanent play with the order of events and, in his latest productions, with plausibility and History (with capital letter). Let's think, too, of the continuous breakdowns of the "fourth wall", the stamp that Phoebe Waller-Bridge put on her magnificent *Fleabag* series. Or, without going too far, in Christopher Nolan and his screenplay of *Oppenheimer* written in the first person. The literary form of the screenplay is, as can be seen, constantly evolving. And, much to the chagrin of Robert McKee – or the Robert McKee played by the now very famous Brian Cox in *Adaptation* – the form has the virtue of emancipating itself even from the heavy tradition of the central conflict (that tradition that our Raúl Ruiz repudiated in order to vindicate, instead, the *poetics* of cinema).

The crossovers between literature and cinema are too vast to be confined in these hurried paragraphs. Marguerite Duras played on both fronts; so did Susan Sontag for a while. Note that Tarantino turned his screenplay for *Once Upon a Time in Hollywood* into a novel in its own right; while Almodóvar published his screenplay for *The Skin I Live In* with the prestigious publishing house Anagrama. Cinematographic structure and in particular, montage, has spread throughout novelistic writing—think, for example, of Vargas Llosa's early work—as much as narrative has flooded the screens. Here, in a hurry, the work of Wes Anderson comes to me, from *The Royal Tenenbaums* onwards, and who takes the transfer of styles to its extreme in his recent adaptations of Roald Dahl's short stories. And how can we not remember the final scene of *The Sheltering Sky*, by Bernardo Bertolucci, in which it is the author himself, Paul Bowles, who recites – looking at the camera – one of the most penetrating phrases of his novel of the same name.

Three

We could go on like this for days. The truth is that cinema is a strange phantasmagoria. Just as it feeds on the literature of all times, it also breathes life into new writings; if, as has been said, you write what you see, today, you see how you film. (Or so it was, at least, during the reign of the analogous. The man with the camera replaced the eye.)

It is clear, then, that the screenplay is a literary form. And just as we gladly accept the reading of theatre, we should also accept the reading of cinema. Let's think about it with a practical example. I don't know about you, but I've never seen a Sophocles play live. Oedipus and Antigone, for example, I have read and analyzed (they must be the most over-analyzed works in Western literature), but I have not seen them represented. It must be impressive; they say that the depiction of Greek tragedy was very similar to what today has come to be called an "immersive" experience, particularly because it had a strong component of political ritual. But I, at least, have not experienced it. Does that stop you from enjoying your reading of them? Not at all, because it is the plot – the *mythos* – and its sharp dialogues that prevail.

With these analogies, I do not want to elevate the text we have here to the maximum power. It is not fair for anyone to face such indisputable names as Sophocles (or Tarantino in movies). Even less so for a first-time writer. Certainly, the reader will have qualms with this or that idea, they will imagine the dialogues differently in their own heads, they will try to understand the events by their own standards. They will even imagine a completely different ending. Well, that's what it's all about. This is the leap of faith that we talked about at the beginning. But more than a leap of faith, it's a *leap of imagination*. This is a potential film. The reader is asked to fill in the intermediate points, to imagine the film without having an existing product as an obligatory reference. Each reader will thus construct the film in his or her head. By the end of this exercise, there will be as many movies as there are readers of this book. And, perhaps, one day, one of them will take it from the world of fantasy to the world of reality (paying, of course, the corresponding royalties).

Víctor Soto Martínez
Santiago, October 2023

Post credit scene

Italo Calvino imagined invisible cities. Let's hope that, with this publication, a trend of imagining – paradox among paradoxes – *invisible films* will begin.

"The laws of physics exist only to convince us of what we think we are incapable of."

- Dr. Ainhoa C.C.

1 **INT. TV SET, TALK-SHOW ATALAYA - NIGHT**   1

   The deep, tired breathing of 90-year-old Elena can be heard
   in the darkness.

   Among the shadows, on the floor you can see a table lamp that
   is flickering, as if about to explode. A red-labeled bottle
   of red wine is lying next to a broken glass that's still
   dripping, feeding a small puddle of the same wine that looks
   like a pool of blood.

   A small coffee table is completely upside down with a broken
   leg, a cheese and fruit board is strewn all over the floor,
   and a fraction of a red neon sign with the letters "AT"
   colors the atmosphere.

   TV cue cards are scattered on the side of the table with the
   logo of the show "Atalaya" and a ball of green yarn is lying
   on the floor, half-disassembled, with no beginning or end.

   Elena's painted lips show traces of a cleft palate. She
   smiles and you can see some very white and well-kept teeth.
   Her blue eyes sparkle with excitement, behind huge golden
   optical lenses.

   Elena is standing, leaning on her thin wooden cane. She takes
   a step forward, takes a couple of deep breaths, and calms
   down. She tucks her short hair and shakes the dust off her
   long and elegant light gray cardigan that reveals her
   lavalier microphone.

                          ELENA
                Who would I be if at this point in
                my life, at this precise place in
                time, I wasn't willing to accept
                the risks I'm going to take?

   A little further back, on the floor and in pain, behind
   everything and near a panel that simulates a large wooden
   window with a night city printed on paper, is INTI (35 years
   old), the host of the show, who seems to have been very
   dressed up only a few minutes ago. He rubs his face. His nose
   is broken and bleeding. He wears a large, light flannel shirt
   that also has his lavalier microphone hooked on.

   He gets up little by little until he is standing. He grabs
   hold of an unlit spotlight, the kind that should be behind
   the camera to illuminate the set. He stands aloof, looking at
   Elena, perplexed.

Elena clears her throat. She stands firm and with a straight back. Now she is ready. She addresses the camera, the viewing audience, and speaks in a confident tone, as if it were a speech prepared for a long time.

> ELENA
> My name is Elena Grajales and today, Monday, June 8, 1998... I am lucky enough to be able to be here, with you.

Elena looks at Inti in the eyes.

> ELENA
> And for you, Inti, I will prove what we all thought impossible.

Elena checks her analog wristwatch, one that is clearly very old and has a leather strap, with many details on it.

> ELENA
> Without further ado, against all possible questioning, here and now, in front of all of you..., I, Elena Grajales, will travel back in time..., and I will accept all the consequences that this decision and this trip may cause.

A sepulchral silence ensues. Inti just looks at her, expectant.

> ELENA
> In 3... It's all worth it at this point.

Inti is going to say something, but he holds back. He approaches Elena slowly until she looks at him and he stops in his tracks. Elena stares at him until Inti decides to take a step back. Elena continues.

> ELENA
> 2... Because I finally know that this is what it should have always been.

Elena squeezes her cane firmly.

> ELENA
> (whispering)
> Who would I be if I didn't do everything I could to be happy beside my family?

Inti smiles and Elena smiles again. She stands tall and self-assured.

Elena looks at the camera, then at Inti and...

She presses the only button on her watch.

Inti takes a step further closer to Elena.

Elena's eyes fill with emotion.

                                                    CUT TO:

2 **INT. TV SET, TALK-SHOW ATALAYA - NIGHT**   2

Opening credits.

All dark. The opening credits of the film "A Patient on Atalaya or Elena and the First Time Travel in History" appear.

Little by little it intermingles with the animated logo of the show "Atalaya", until only the logo of the show remains.

It is viewed through a large television with built-in VHS, presenting the beginning of the show, with introductory instrumental music. Below, in overlapping and smaller letters: "with Jorge Enrique 'Inti' Rogers."

3 **EXT. CHANNEL BUILDING FAÇADE - NIGHT**   3

A building with huge satellite dishes on its roof. Cars drive through the city streets.

                    INTI (S.O.)
          Hello, good evening everyone, my
          name is Jorge Enrique Rogers... or
          "Inti," as most people know me
          today.

4 **INT. TV SET, TALK-SHOW ATALAYA - NIGHT**   4

It is a two-tiered study. On the lowest level there are two armchairs with a coffee table between them. Further back, there is the same television that permanently displays an animation with the show's logo, next to a landline phone. And next to the large fake window showing a printed image of the city at night, there is a red neon sign with the show's name.

                    INTI (S.O.)
          It is exactly 10 PM on Monday, June
          8th and from the depths of our
          channel "two and a half", I welcome
          you to a new chapter of "Atalaya".

Inti is alone, sitting in an armchair in front of the coffee table.

Now he smiles very kindly at the camera, he is very well dressed, his hair perfectly styled, very well groomed and tidy. He modulates very noticeably.

                    INTI
          In previous chapters we have talked
          about esotericism, astral travel,
          contact with the afterlife,
          hypnosis with the great expert from
          Chilean television and UFOs, with
          the show that is being prepared for
          next year, the old story of the
          Valdés Case and even the alleged
          abductions of celebrities. We have
          also dabbled in conspiracy theories
          about the end of the world and the
          inevitable arrival of the new
          millennium. Of course, these are
          complex issues, but as always,
          difficulty will not prevent us from
          fulfilling our mission of seeking
          the truth... or getting as close to
          it as we can.

A DARK-HAIRED PRODUCTION ASSISTANT approaches, sets down a bottle of blue-labeled wine and two glasses on the coffee table, and fills one of them. Inti takes it.

                    INTI
          On this occasion and on the eve of
          the World Cup in France, I tell you
          that we will NOT be talking about
          soccer.

A recorded boo is heard.

                    INTI
          But don't worry, this is much more
          interesting... While all the rest
          of Chilean television is dedicated
          to that, we have an interesting
          challenge in our search for the
          truth.

He raises his wine glass.

                    INTI
          And as always, to find the truth,
          we have a new and excellent export
          wine, especially brought to this
          show to allow us to let go of all
          kinds of inhibitions.

Inti smiles and makes a toast gesture to the camera.

                    INTI
          What could be better than a good
          conversation over a good wine?

Inti pauses to taste the wine. He makes a gesture of
disapproval and disgust.

                    INTI
          I don't just say it's good wine
          because it's the only sponsorship
          we have.

Inti laughs and reacts to gestures made behind the scenes.

                    INTI
          I know it's good wine and I'm not
          just saying that because it's a
          gift to us.

He continues to laugh and takes another forced drink.

                    INTI
          Today we have a special gentleman
          as a guest...

Looks behind the scenes again.

                    INTI
          I'm sorry, I'm sorry. We have a
          very special LADY as a guest. It's
          just that there were some last
          minute changes, apologies. Not only
          does she want to tell us something
          completely unbelievable, but she
          also says that she can convince us
          that she... It's almost impossible
          to say this in a way that doesn't
          sound crazy, so I'll get straight
          to the point: she claims to have
          built a time machine.

He smiles and lets a few seconds pass for the guest intro
jingle to finish.

                    INTI
          You heard that right! Our guest
          today claims to have built a time
          machine and comes to convince us
          that time travel is possible! How
          will she do it? Welcome once again
          to another episode of "Atalaya."
          And especially, let's welcome Mrs.
          Elena Grajales, who claims to be
          the creator of the first- and sole-
          time machine... in history!

Recorded applause is heard in addition to the introductory
music. Inti smiles mockingly and laughter from the production
team can be heard in the background.

Elena enters slowly, cane in hand, neatly coiffed and
elegant. She's very nervous and doesn't take her eyes off
Inti.

When she reaches his side, Inti holds out his hand to greet
her and she extends hers, trembling. Inti notices.

                    INTI
          Don't worry, I'm just a regular
          person. It's okay.

Elena smiles and decides to hug him. Inti allows this quite
calmly, until he determines that a lot of time has passed. He
smiles kindly and pulls away from her.

Elena looks at him with teary eyes and sits in the armchair
in front of him.

Inti offers her a glass of wine and Elena happily accepts,
immediately taking a long sip. She sets the glass down on the
table and stares at Inti.

                    INTI
          A pleasure to meet you, Mrs.
          Elena...

                    ELENA
          The pleasure is mine, Inti... I
          thank you deeply for having me and
          for the opportunity to be here with
          you today on this show. I couldn't
          wait to meet you.

                    INTI
          Of course, don't worry. With what
          you are coming to tell us, it is
          certainly a pleasure to have you on
          our show.

Elena smiles shyly.

> INTI
> Mrs. Elena, as you well know, and I think it's something that you've already discussed with the production, the idea is that you tell us your story and help us find the truth in it.

> ELENA
> I know.

> INTI
> Finding the truth whatever it is, whether we like it or not.

Elena doesn't answer.

> INTI
> We know that it can be something complex, since it is impossible for us to start a conversation of this sort immediately believing that what you say is true... I don't know if I'm explaining myself properly.

Elena still doesn't respond, so Inti looks behind the camera not knowing what to do.

As if following instructions, he refills Elena's glass.

Elena takes another long sip of wine. She stares at the glass.

> ELENA
> Can you repeat the question please, Inti?

> INTI
> It wasn't really a question, but rather a comment, hoping that you can clarify the situation for me.

> ELENA
> What situation?

> INTI
> Come on, Mrs. Elena, please.

Elena's left hand doesn't stop shaking, so she positions her right hand over it to calm down.

ELENA
Do you enjoy being the host of this show? Are you happy with this job?

INTI
Yes, of course! What is there to dislike? Of course I'm also looking forward to trying new things, but I love what I do. Don't you like the show? Maybe we're... too nerdy for you?

Recorded laughter is heard.

ELENA
No, not at all. It's not that I don't like it. Of course I like it, of course.

INTI
Good to know!

ELENA
It's that your goal is to seek the truth in subjects where it's very difficult to find it.

INTI
That's exactly what I love. Don't you think it's exciting? It's like discovering something new every day.

ELENA
If you actually figure it out. These are not easy subjects.

INTI
And if we don't find out the truth, at least we can get as close to it as possible. And I can be glad I tried for it. No problem. Isn't that all it takes? To at least try?

ELENA
I thought "all it took" was to find the truth.

INTI
Well, there's always an answer, but sometimes it's... no more than a sham... Lies. And the audience doesn't always like that response.

I may not even like it, which has happened to me a lot lately. But that's what we're here for. To seek the truth even if it's just once a week.

Silence. Elena takes a swig of her wine.

                    ELENA
It was basically unintentional.

                    INTI
What was?

                    ELENA
How I figured out how to travel through time.

                    INTI
Unintentional? What do you mean?

                    ELENA
Some of the most important discoveries in history have happened unintentionally, or by accident, looking for something else.

                    INTI
Yes, I understand that there are very particular cases...

                    ELENA
Well, this is one of them, then.

                    INTI
Just like that? Isn't there any explanation other than that?

                    ELENA
Not one that is relevant at this point.

                    INTI
Well... then?

Inti waits, but Elena doesn't give any more information.

                    INTI
And where is it that you have supposedly gone to, so far? To what times and places? To the past, to the future?

                    ELENA
          No... I haven't traveled yet.

Inti laughs, uncomfortable.

                    INTI
          What? So how are you supposed to
          know the time machine works? We
          haven't gotten off to a very good
          start, I must say.

                    ELENA
          I've done some testing, of course.

                    INTI
          Sure, of course, you did some
          tests.

Elena doesn't answer. She's still very shy.

                    INTI
          Perhaps if you expand a little
          further and tell us something not
          so abridged?

                    ELENA
          What else can I say?

                    INTI
          That's what you came for, right? To
          prove that time travel is possible.

                    ELENA
          Not really. I came to meet you.

                    INTI
          The truth is that I am very
          flattered, but I must mention that
          I am madly in love with my wife.

Inti shows his wedding ring to Elena. Laughter and applause can be heard in the background.

                    ELENA
          I didn't mean it like that. Of
          course not.

Inti smiles.

                    INTI
          Of course not.

> ELENA
> Proving time travel is simply an extra advantage to being here today, and the perfect way to get to meet you, even if it's just for a moment. Also, in some way I think my presence in the show helps you.

> INTI
> You could help me a lot, as long as your story is true.

> ELENA
> Of course.

> INTI
> And how does the machine work? Does it use plutonium, renewable energy, garbage?

Inti is utterly sarcastic. Elena ignores him.

> INTI
> Nothing explosive, right?

Silence.

Elena shows him the watch.

> INTI
> Are you going to tell me that you can travel back in time with a simple watch?

Inti looks behind the camera again, as if looking for an explanation from the producers. Why is Elena sitting there with him on the show?

> ELENA
> Why should it only be possible with a big machine? Isn't a watch more practical and functional?

> INTI
> Seriously? Just like that, because of the practicality and functionality?

Elena shrugs.

> INTI
> I don't know if you know, but today we had another special guest scheduled: José Mella.

Elena winces disapprovingly. She doesn't care who José Mella is.

> INTI
> José Mella, a chemical engineer who, for whatever reasons, ended up devoting himself to being a medium. Are you going to tell me you don't know him? He became famous when he allegedly managed to contact José Artigas, in a live show in Uruguay... I think he gave information about his life that was not known at the time, which was later verified... He's gotten quite popular after that...

> ELENA
> I'm sorry...

> INTI
> Seriously? He has broken records as a medium and as a speaker everywhere. Every show he has is sold out! A true rockstar! He has traveled all over the world giving lectures and has a busy schedule for about 6 or 8 more months now. And what's more, he doesn't come cheap at all!

He thinks about it for a few seconds.

> INTI
> Actually, he HAD a busy schedule. Now I guess it will depend on the investigation.

Elena takes a sip of wine without saying anything.

> INTI
> Just today he was arrested for allegedly carrying explosive devices... Can you believe it? Who's going to come to this show carrying explosives? Least of all him... What for?

Inti takes a sip of wine.

> INTI
> Although I shouldn't talk too much about this topic while it's under investigation...

> My point is that only just today…, well…, you invited yourself, didn't you?

Elena smiles.

> ELENA
> Thank you very much for the clarification.

> INTI
> Of course, after the insistence and now the accusation against José, all at the last minute, it was a real pleasure to welcome you on our show.

Elena and Inti smile together, accomplices.

> INTI
> What I mean, is that it usually takes a long time to schedule a guest. I guess it was fortunate for you that José was cancelled at the last minute.

> ELENA
> I guess José will need a bit of luck with that kind of trouble...

> INTI
> Come on, I can't talk about this anymore, you are killing me! So, I would appreciate it if you would please help me by answering some of my questions. Tell our loyal audience, who is Elena Grajales and why do you think you can travel in time?

> ELENA
> Well, I'm a psychologist and a teacher... Or I was, at least, until I retired and went about my own things... quite a few years ago.

> INTI
> What things?

> ELENA
> That is beside the point.

> INTI
> There seems to be no point! Come on Mrs. Elena, a little help. Did psychology or teaching… help you create a so-called time machine?

> ELENA
> From a psychological point of view, many questions can arise about how time affects human beings and their stages in development. I imagine it may have helped me with more than a few things... And in a sense, if you think about it, all psychologists are time travelers in some way.

Inti laughs.

> INTI
> How so?

> ELENA
> We must go back, dig into the past and even change the perception of it...

> INTI
> But in terms of perception.

> ELENA
> Most of life is perception.

> INTI
> But that doesn't have repercussions in the future, so it's really not the same.

> ELENA
> Of course it has repercussions. These changes, when well conducted by the psychologist, are gradually reflected in the present and in the future. The person changes, therefore, their life changes.

> INTI
> That's great... but let's see, Mrs. Elena... Come on, please... let's get to the point... How were you able to create a time machine?... Or rather, that watch?

> Because I think that when you told us that you were able to travel in time, you weren't referring to that in psychological terms, were you?

Elena is calmer again. She takes a drink of wine and stares at the glass.

> ELENA
> Excellent wine. It's been a long time since I've had it. Carménère?

> INTI
> Merlot.

Inti picks up the bottle and looks at it.

> INTI
> Oh no, you're right. CARMERENE. Good palate.

Inti sighs, takes a long sip of wine imitating Elena and continues.

> INTI
> You know?... It's very hard to believe what you say...

> ELENA
> What?

> INTI
> That your watch is a time machine.

> ELENA
> Oh, right. I know. That's why I brought it.

Elena moves her arm close to him to show him the watch. Inti observes it.

> INTI
> Uff, you can tell that it took a lot of work.

The watch is small, analogous and made of gold, with a single button on the side. The strap of the watch is made of leather and is ridiculously thick compared to the size of the watch itself. It has a certain pattern, as if it were filled with a web of cables that cross it from side to side.

                    INTI
          Come on... Explain it a little, how
          do you intend to prove that time
          travel is possible... with a watch?

                    ELENA
          The easiest way is to travel back
          in time.

Inti looks at her blankly.

                    INTI
          How? Will you be traveling right
          now, on the show? On Atalaya?

Elena looks at her watch.

                    ELENA
          Yes. That's enough.

5   **INT. TIMELESS ROOM - DAY**   5

OVERLAY TEXT: Name: Virginia, Age: 9 years, Year: 1997.

A SCHOOL GIRL is sitting in front of the camera, on a huge, vintage-style sofa. The wall behind the sofa has wallpaper with designs and drawings reminiscent of the ancient Greeks.

Next to the sofa is a long vase with a bouquet of pompous yellow flowers. On the other side there is a record player from which Mozart can be heard (Piano Concerto N° 21).

It is a place and an environment that is difficult to define in terms of time.

The light coming in through to the sofa seems to pass through blinds.

The girl wears a school uniform and carries a backpack. She has her feet crossed on the couch and is playing with a virtual pet. She has a cleft palate.

She takes a breath to speak. She finishes feeding her virtual pet and sets it aside to address the camera.

                    SCHOOL GIRL
          Although I'm not of legal age yet
          and I have a long way to go for
          that, if I could travel back in
          time, the first thing I would do is
          go back in time to prevent time
          travel from being invented. I think
          it's too great a power for anyone.

Her virtual pet rings. The girl looks at it, smiles, and decides to continue with what she was saying.

> SCHOOL GIRL
> You can't play with people's lives. If pharmacies plot together for their own benefit at the expense of the health of all Chileans, imagine what they would do if they had the power to travel back in time.

The virtual pet rings again. She looks at it, picks it up and decides to play with it again, while smiling.

She looks at the camera again.

> SCHOOL GIRL
> That's what I would do. And if I were older, I think I would have to do the same. Or maybe I shouldn't travel at all... Adults can't be trusted.

6 **INT. TV SET, TALK-SHOW ATALAYA - EVENING** 6

The conversation between Inti and Elena continues. Inti remains incredulous and sarcastic.

> INTI
> What do you need me to do so that you can travel? How can I help you?

Elena hesitates and begins to search within her purse.

> ELENA
> I guess I can stay a little longer. Just a little bit more.

> INTI
> Of course. Why not, right?

She finds an envelope and hands it to Inti, who opens it and begins to read.

> ELENA
> Like I said, I came to meet you, Inti, so we can wait a little bit longer.

When Inti understands what he is reading, he looks at Elena without saying anything. Inti takes his seat again. Elena smiles.

                         INTI
               I don't understand.

Inti looks at Elena expectantly, the document in his hand.

                         INTI
               What is this?

Inti shakes the document in front of Elena while she can't help but smile. Elena sits across from him.

                         ELENA
               I didn't get to meet my biological
               father, because he passed away
               before I was born. My mother never
               got over his death and took her own
               life, so I grew up with another
               family. They educated me, gave me a
               place to sleep, food, and took care
               of me as if I were their own
               daughter.

Silence. They both take a long swig of wine. Inti watches her without saying anything.

                         INTI
               I'm so sorry, I really am.

                         ELENA
               I've thought about it a lot. And
               while I'm so grateful for what they
               did with my life... of all that
               they have done for me...

                         INTI
               But this... Let's see..., wait...

Inti stands up.

                         INTI
               With this, are you telling me that
               you came from the future?

Inti looks at the camera, as if wanting to explain to his audience.

                         INTI
               This is an alleged DNA test from
               the future... which basically says
               that Mrs. Elena here...

He looks towards Elena.

                        INTI
            You... ARE MY DAUGHTER.

Humorous music is played.

                        INTI
            Let's see... For that to be true,
            you would have to come from the
            future...

                        ELENA
            With all that my adoptive family
            did for me, I've never been able to
            stop thinking about what would have
            happened if I could save my
            father's life. If I could save
            you...

                        INTI
            I'm sorry, but you're going to have
            to explain a lot more than that if
            you want me to believe any of this.
            We have never seen this before in
            Atalaya!

Inti takes a deep breath and becomes serious again.

                        INTI
            Let's start from the beginning...
            What did your father die from, Mrs.
            Elena?

Long silence. Elena goes to raise the glass of wine, but because of her nerves she topples the bottle and it falls to the floor. Elena gets upset.

                        ELENA
            Excuse me, sorry... I didn't mean
            to...

The dark brown haired production assistant comes over and starts cleaning and tidying up quickly.

                        INTI
            Don't worry. A guest came here with
            a dog, once. And you can imagine
            that the table is just the height
            of a Border Collie's tail... It was
            only a matter of time.

Elena smiles and gives silent thanks for the calming down.

                    INTI
          And it wasn't just once, not just
          one thing... The dog couldn't stand
          us sitting still for a second...

                    ELENA
          Thank you.

                    INTI
          He was supposed to be grown,
          mature, and trained.

                    ELENA
          Maybe he just wanted to eat
          something. Or maybe, I don't
          know... I've read that it's also a
          way to get attention, like
          children.

Silence.

                    INTI
          Sorry. So, what did your father die
          from, Mrs. Elena?

                    ELENA
          What really matters isn't what he
          died from. The important thing for
          me was to know if I could do
          something about it.

                    INTI
          Save him.

Elena nods, embarrassed.

                    INTI
          Sure, but I'm assuming that one
          thing is significant for the
          other...

Elena carefully picks up her glass.

                    INTI
          Would you like a glass of water?

                    ELENA
          Oh, no. It's ok.

Inti gestures to the production crew and they put a glass of
water next to her wine glass as well as another closed
bottle.

                    ELENA
          Can you leave the bottle open
          anyways?

Inti is uncomfortable, but nods looking behind the camera and
the assistant arrives to uncork the bottle.

                    ELENA
          I'm not drunk, you know? I have an
          impressive liver.

                    INTI
          Now that's something we have in
          common.

They both laugh.

                    ELENA
          Sorry. I'm just nervous.

                    INTI
          I can imagine, it must not be easy
          to believe that you are a time
          traveler, that you come from the
          future, and that I am your father.

Inti shakes the paper again. Elena looks at him annoyed. That
was clearly not what she meant.

                    ELENA
          Of course.

                    INTI
          Well then?

                    ELENA
          An interesting thing that happens
          regarding time travel, at least
          when you know it's possible, is
          that you have to start thinking
          about the real possibilities above
          all.

                    INTI
          What do you mean?

                    ELENA
          The actual possibilities are very
          different from the hypothetical
          possibilities...

                    INTI
          For example?

ELENA
For example, what would you do if you could save a life right now?

INTI
If I could, of course I'd save it.

ELENA
Of course you save a life, yes. If you travel back in time, you will be in another moment that you will consider as a new "here and now". So, you need to consider beforehand whether you want to save that life or not.

INTI
Sure, I understand.

ELENA
What is morally correct?

INTI
Okay, okay, but that moment is over.

ELENA
For you. Not for them. The very concept that something "has already happened" is based on the idea that time is inevitable. But that changes when you can travel back in time and make new decisions about it.

INTI
So, are you convinced of this?

ELENA
Of course.

INTI
I mean, are you convinced with this whole story? That it is true that you can travel back in time and you can also save me from something seemingly inevitable?

ELENA
Yes, of course.

INTI
Absolutely sure?

> ELENA
> Absolutely.

Inti stands up and walks towards the camera, holding up the letter Elena gave him.

> INTI
> Actually, I'm sorry, but there's nothing you can do to convince me of this. It just seems too... too... It's not something I could believe without any real proof.

> ELENA
> But this document...

> INTI
> There is no way to verify this, Mrs. Elena.

> ELENA
> It's official.

Inti looks back at the camera.

> INTI
> Well, if so, and with all due respect, the alleged fact that this is a DNA test of the future that indicates that you are my daughter and that you are coming to save me, would imply that you lied to us from the beginning, since you said that you had not time traveled before. Then you have changed your speech. And as the saying goes: "he who tells the truth, does not lie, or at least, does not need to."

> ELENA
> I didn't really think that I would share this information with you... It wasn't necessary to change history and besides, you wouldn't have believed me.

> INTI
> Nor do I now. Let's face it, what kind of document that has a date in the future could be considered real?

Elena is uncomfortable.

INTI
I know that sounds exciting, yes. But we have to be objective. We've seen weird things in this show and this is just another weird thing. And it doesn't even qualify as something weird. It's more of a simple lie, no offense intended. Is... It's just another sham...

Inti takes a sip of wine.

ELENA
The document is legitimate, official, and one hundred percent real.

INTI
It looks legit. But that's it. The date is... about 90 years in the future.

ELENA
That's right.

INTI
How's that? You're going to tell me that you're over 90 years old?

ELENA
90 years old, precisely.

INTI
I really don't believe that! If so, I congratulate you!

Elena smiles gratefully.

ELENA
Well, it's true. Thank you.

Silence.

ELENA
Is your wife pregnant?

Inti breathes in deeply.

INTI
That's not proof of anything.

ELENA
Of course it is.

                    INTI
          And what do we do with that
          information? Is that baby supposed
          to be you?

                    ELENA
          Why not?

                    INTI
          Seriously?

Silence.

                    INTI
          Plus, our baby is a boy. A MALE. We
          only found out yesterday and
          apparently that information has not
          yet reached the press.

                    ELENA
          What? It's a boy?

                    INTI
          We were told yesterday.

                    ELENA
          Who told you? But she's only just
          pregnant... How can they tell? ...
          No, they can't be one hundred
          percent sure...

                    INTI
          With today's technology, you can
          know.

                    ELENA
          But sometimes they're wrong, aren't
          they? They're not 100 percent sure
          he's a boy... It's too early to be
          sure.

                    INTI
          Look, I'm sorry. Even if it was,
          "Elena" was never a choice of a
          name for our child.

Silence. They both drink from their glasses to calm down.

                    INTI
          His name will be Carlos, like my
          grandfather.

Inti tucks away the document into one of his pockets.

                    INTI
          And when we thought she might be a
          woman, we thought of Raquel, but
          not Elena.

Elena doesn't answer.

                    INTI
          I am sorry. "Elena" was simply
          never an option.

                    ELENA
          But that could change if you... You
          die and eventually the baby is put
          up for adoption.

                    INTI
          Let's see. If it's a girl and not a
          boy, as the professionals told us,
          then my wife and I die, and the
          girl who doesn't have a name yet is
          adopted by another family... Within
          that one-million-in-a-million
          possibility... no, in a billion or
          more, much more— I suppose the
          people who adopt her could name her
          Elena.

                    ELENA
          That must be it...

                    INTI
          Also, how did you get a DNA test
          from your father, if he was
          supposed to have died before you
          were born?

                    ELENA
          I guess it sounds very difficult to
          achieve something like that in this
          day and age...

                    INTI
          I don't know. I really have no
          idea. But why didn't you bring a
          DNA test taken in these times?
          Something we can use; with names of
          real people we can contact.

                    ELENA
          I understand that nowadays it's not
          that easy...

> Also, I would probably need your approval, and the DNA test was something I needed for myself. To be completely sure of what I was doing. I never thought it would be necessary to show it to you. Believe me, I considered it, but I didn't have time for all this...

Inti bursts out laughing.

> **INTI**
> Time? The time traveler didn't have time... And you say you need my approval for a DNA test. Didn't you need my approval in the future?

> **ELENA**
> As I told you, in the future you are dead.

> **INTI**
> True, true. How convenient.

> **ELENA**
> No, not really. Not at all.

Elena looks at her watch and stands up.

> **ELENA**
> I think enough is enough.

> **INTI**
> Enough for what?

> **ELENA**
> To travel and show you that I am your daughter.

> **INTI**
> Just like that?

Inti stands up as well and follows her, smiling anxiously and incredulously.

> **INTI**
> I would have imagined that anyone who could create a time machine would hide it. Why come and present it to the world? And why here, in this modest show, and in Chile?

> **ELENA**
> Why not?

                    INTI
          I don't know, maybe because we're
          used to these things happening in
          New York or something.

                    ELENA
          That's fiction. I'm talking about
          something real.

                    INTI
          Until you prove it, it will remain
          fiction.

Elena looks at her watch and then grabs her cane.

                    ELENA
          Do you want me to travel or not?

                    INTI
          Right here? Right now?

                    ELENA
          Of course. That's what I came here
          for.

                    INTI
          So, you did come to prove that time
          travel is possible.

Elena grabs her cane with both hands and walks over to the camera. Inti looks at her nervously and behind the camera the crew signal to him.

                    INTI
          Wait, wait, please.

                    ELENA
          We'll have time.

                    INTI
          Wait, please. Before we go any
          further. I must be cautious... And
          I must ask just one more question
          before you travel.

Elena turns and looks at him, waiting for Inti to continue.

                    INTI
          What should we expect, if you can
          indeed travel back in time?... Are
          you going to disappear and come
          back? Can't you see there is quite
          a bit of show left...

> What are we supposed to do next if you don't come back?... What are you going to do? What's going to happen now?

> ELENA
> I'm going to travel back in time to change my story... And we will definitely see each other again.

Inti falls silent.

> INTI
> Wait, wait!

Inti gets up and positions himself next to Elena.

> INTI
> It's just that I want to be by your side when... when you try.

> ELENA
> Not so close, please.

Inti pulls away from her, intimidated.

> INTI
> Is it safe here?

> ELENA
> I guess.

Inti frowns and worriedly takes one more step back.

> INTI
> Please. Proceed.

He gestures with his hands for Elena to continue. Elena clenches her cane tightly and looks up, fully erect.

> ELENA
> Thank you, Inti, for everything...

They smile at each other.

> ELENA
> Today, here and now, in front of all of you..., I, Elena Grajales, will travel back in time...

Elena fixes her hair.

> ELENA
> In 3...

Inti takes a deep breath.

                   ELENA
    Two...

Elena brings her watch close to her face to get a better look at it.

                   INTI
    Do you think there is a risk of
    death?

Silence.

                   ELENA
    Believe me, WITH ME there is no
    risk of death here.

Elena continues almost incomprehensibly. Inti takes a step back.

                   ELENA
        (whispering)
    One...

Elena presses the only button on her watch.

A deep sound begins to grow, and the lights begin to flicker. The sound gradually increases until:

BOOOOOOOOM!

A thunderous noise saturates the entire space.

Inti falls to the floor in fright. The lights in the studio begin to burst one by one until it is almost completely dark. The only light left on is that of the lamp on the coffee table, barely enough to make their faces noticeable, and it flickers erratically.

Suddenly, the metallic sound stops, everything is silent for a few seconds. Inti and Elena are absolutely still, until...

PAF! The lamp on the coffee table explodes and everything goes completely dark.

                                        CUT TO BLACK.

7 **INT. TIMELESS ROOM - DAY** 7

OVERLAY TEXT: Name: Alejandro, Age: 46 years, Year: 1975.

A PHOTOGRAPHER is sitting in front of the camera, in the same living room and on the same huge, vintage-style couch.

On the record player, we continue listening to Mozart (Piano Sonata N° 16 in C Major).

The man wears a gray jacket and pants and a blue shirt with the last button open and a large collar. He has long hair and sideburns. He looks very neat. A camera hangs from his neck.

He is smoking and throws the ashes into the stone ashtray next to the vase. The cigarette in his mouth reveals that he also has a cleft palate.

He's relaxed, as if he's been thinking about the answer for a long time. He's cross-legged and lying down, searching for the right words.

The man speaks, looking behind the camera.

> PHOTOGRAPHER
> Can I take whatever I want?

The man nods, as if he has heard the answer.

> PHOTOGRAPHER
> It's a complex question... But in the end... I think... Yes. If I could travel back in time, even once, I would definitely leave this place.

He smokes, throws away the ashes from his cigarette, and thinks for a few more seconds before continuing.

> PHOTOGRAPHER
> I would find a quiet place to go with my wife and children. I have two kids and... I would like them to live quietly, in a place like...

He looks through the camera lens. He's checking that everything is working perfectly.

> PHOTOGRAPHER
> I would travel to Italy. I would go back to the best times of olive oil, of the famous liquid gold. I would take advantage of my knowledge of the future to make enough to live and educate my children there. Nothing more than that, just what's necessary.

>   We would live peacefully, in a
>   small vineyard that would give us
>   enough to live well and drink a
>   good wine. And everyone would be
>   invited to celebrate with us
>   whenever they want.

He pauses and smokes.

>   PHOTOGRAPHER
>   Think about it, an incredible
>   landscape and an extraordinary life
>   with those you love the most... And
>   of course, I'd take my camera and
>   document it all.

He stubs out his cigarette and removes the cap from his camera lens.

>   PHOTOGRAPHER
>   Imagine what it would be like for
>   my children to grow up with those
>   memories...

He points his lens directly at the camera, at those interviewing him and click! the shutter is heard.

He smiles as he sits checking his camera. He turns the knob of the camera roll leaving it ready for a next photo.

8 **INT. TV SET, TALK-SHOW ATALAYA - NIGHT**   8

The table lamp light turns on. A BLOND PRODUCTION ASSISTANT is squeezing in a new light bulb. Other lights come back on, but everything remains dim, nothing like the initial illumination.

Elena moves desperately from side to side, walking with her cane, which now has a metal head, and drinks an entire glass of wine. The blond production assistant approaches the table again to fill the glasses. He arrives with a bottle of wine that now has a white label.

>   INTI
>   I know it's unfortunate, but...

>   ELENA
>   Unfortunate? This is not
>   unfortunate. It's something much
>   worse...

INTI
Come on, we can all make mistakes.
We knew this could happen and
you... You also knew this was a
possibility. In fact, it was the
most likely outcome.

ELENA
Sometimes things not working out is
not an option.

Elena continues from side to side, checking her watch and
looking around, as if looking for an answer.

INTI
Please take a seat, Mrs. Elena.

Elena keeps pacing around, worried.

INTI
Please, Mrs. Elena. Let's look for
the answers we both want and...
Let's take the opportunity to get
to know each other a little better.

Elena stops in her tracks.

ELENA
Get to know each other?

INTI
You said you wanted to meet me,
didn't you? And I'm here to get to
know you a little better.

Elena sits down without letting go of her cane.

INTI
Thank you.

Elena falls silent. Inti sighs and continues.

INTI
What's the problem, then? How can I
help you, Mrs. Elena?

Elena looks at him suspiciously. Takes a deep breath.

ELENA
Many years ago, when I was studying
at school, I was lucky enough to
participate in different classes
and plays.

I particularly remember those classes where we had to lie on the floor and shout whatever emotion we felt at the time.

INTI
Who wouldn't want to have those kinds of moments now, right? The ones where we let go of everything. A privilege of being a kid.

ELENA
No doubt. But in addition to screaming emotions, I loved everything that had to do with improvisation. What's more, I was terrible at learning my lines and I always left that part of the work for the end, for the very last minute before presenting the play we were working on.

INTI
It must have been terrible for your classmates.

ELENA
We still had a great time. What I liked most about improvisation was that part where everyone had to follow your idea, or you had to follow theirs. Trusting that the other person in front of you knew what they were doing and what they're saying, even if it's not scripted.

INTI
That doesn't necessarily mean you have to accept everything they say.

ELENA
Of course, it means that. It's exactly what it means.

Inti smiles. He seems to know what Elena is talking about.

ELENA
I would like to ask you to put yourself in my position for a moment, Inti. Even if you don't believe anything I say, I want to ask you to pretend you do, without judging me. Please.

> I simply ask you to play improv for a moment, let yourself be carried away by the emotion and open yourself to the possibility...

Inti doesn't answer.

> ELENA
> For a moment, have a little faith.

> INTI
> We are here precisely in search of something a little more concrete than faith.

> ELENA
> Pretend then, even if it's just for a moment. If you want to help me, that's exactly what I need now.

> INTI
> I opened myself up to the possibility and nothing happened. No more than the lights going out. An impressive trick; Especially considering that you did it with a simple watch. But that has nothing to do with time travel. It was interference or something. I'm sorry, I want to help you, but don't ask me to believe in something that you haven't been able to prove.

> ELENA
> It's just a game, Inti... I need to understand why the watch didn't work. Do you really think it was just interference and nothing more?

> INTI
> Do you really believe that you can travel back in time and that you are my daughter?

Inti takes a swig from his glass. He sees that Elena's glass is empty and refills it.

> INTI
> OK, OK. Let's do the exercise... But you know that an actual demonstration will always be the definitive answer. "To see is to believe."

They both smile. Elena is grateful for the opportunity.

> **INTI**
> Then, we will put ourselves in the situation where time travel is real, and that you know how to travel.

> **ELENA**
> Thank you.

> **INTI**
> Well. How is this supposed to help you be able to travel back in time? What then follows from this assumption?

> **ELENA**
> As the famous historian Lilia Choca said: "let's recapitulate in order to understand, solve and never repeat again".

> **INTI**
> How did it all start, then?

> **ELENA**
> To begin with, when you discover the way to travel through time, without really knowing how time travel works or its repercussions, you must assume that you will be able to travel ONLY ONCE.
> Therefore, the decision of what to do that one time is very difficult to make.

> **INTI**
> Why could you only travel once?

> **ELENA**
> You can figure out afterwards what to do if all goes well.

> **INTI**
> If all goes well?

> **ELENA**
> Of course. It will all depend on how the changes from the first trip affect you.

I can't pretend that I'll be fortunate enough to get there and travel wherever and whenever I want to and as many times as I want. I must start by thinking that I will only be able to do it once.

          INTI
I think I understand.

          ELENA
Plus, there's the issue of age... Whatever I do, I keep getting older... Even if I go back a thousand times to change my eating habits, cure my illnesses or avoid them before they appear or anything else. Whatever I do, time will catch up with me.

She covers her right hand which has begun to quiver.

          INTI
You've thought about it a lot.

          ELENA
Of course.

          INTI
So, as I understand it, the possibilities and the risks are many.

          ELENA
Incalculable. There are risks that you can pretend to control, but others that you simply don't know about. First, you must understand for sure how it works, and for that you have to travel, actually experience it. Because in this case the theory is not enough at all. Therefore, I can only assume that I can travel only once.

          INTI
Very dramatic way of thinking.

          ELENA
Didn't the Wright brothers feel the same way? Maybe their first flight could have been their last...

There are variables and risks that you will only really know in practice... So, did they think about the place where they would fly for the first time? Did they think it really might be their last time as well? Or is it just me who thinks so?

                INTI
Putting myself in the case that time travel is possible... Should I understand then that it is highly risky? Should we be worried if you can finally turn on your watch and manage to travel? After all, the lights thing was quite a show. And if it were true, what else could happen?

Inti smiles. He doesn't believe anything he's saying.

                ELENA
Is any journey not risky? What means of transportation was free from high risk during its invention process?

                INTI
Do you consider it a means of transportation?

                ELENA
I don't see why not. Time travel has been a historical dream, but that doesn't mean it's more than that, a journey.

                INTI
But with effects and consequences.

                ELENA
Quite possibly. Like any trip.

                INTI
Not all travel has consequences as terrible as time travel might. If it were possible to travel back in time, you would have to think very carefully about where and when to travel.

Elena pulls a bag of peanuts out of her purse and puts it on the coffee table.

                    ELENA
          Excuse me, but I don't know how
          many hours have passed since my
          last meal.

Elena hands him the bag of peanuts. Inti takes a handful of peanuts and Elena leaves the bag on the table.

                    INTI
          We usually have dinner with the
          guest before the show and once we
          start, we only have wine. And since
          you arrived unexpectedly...

Elena doesn't say anything.

                    INTI
          I'll see what we can do.

Inti gestures behind the camera.

                    ELENA
          Thank you, Inti.

                    INTI
          A pleasure.

                    ELENA
          So, just as I've questioned myself
          for a long time, I ask the same
          question to you, so you can really
          put yourself in my shoes.

Inti is expectant. Elena, despite talking to Inti, seems to be addressing the viewing audience.

                    ELENA
          If you had the ability to travel
          back in time just once, what would
          you do, where would you go, and
          why?

9 **INT. TIMELESS ROOM - DAY**   9

OVERLAY TEXT: Name: Willian, Age: 35, Year: 2022.

A 35-year-old GROOM looks directly at the camera, sitting on the huge vintage sofa. He dresses formally, but both his blonde hair and his clothes are rather messy, as if he had just arrived from his wedding. He has a cleft palate.

On the record player, Mozart continues to play with "Ave verum corpus".

He wears tight clothing: white shirt, blue pants and vest, along with new brown shoes. He wears a wedding ring on his left hand. He has a face mask on. He takes it off and puts it in his jacket pocket. In addition, he has a bottle of water in his hands.

> GROOM
> I think it was Mahatma Gandhi who once said, "There's more to life than just increasing your speed."

He drinks some water.

> GROOM
> Why is the idea of time travel so appealing? What is it that we crave so much, that we are willing to do anything for it?

He twirls his wedding ring.

> GROOM
> If I could travel back in time, I think I'd worry about not wasting time on so many things that aren't worth it.

He fixes his tie and stares at his ring.

> GROOM
> Maybe I'd go back to yesterday. I would live the day of my wedding again. Over and over again. If I could travel back in time, I would go back and rescue every lost minute and live it to the fullest... Because all good things happen so fast... In the end, nothing is more important than that, right? Rescuing the present?

He stands still, staring into infinity, reflecting.

> GROOM
> Rescuing the present. I like it.

He smiles.

10 **INT. TV SET, TALK-SHOW ATALAYA - NIGHT** 10

Inti and Elena are sitting at a bar-style counter on the side of the set. In front of them, the counter is filled with a cheese and dried fruit and nut board.

In addition, there is a bottle of red wine with a white label and two wine glasses. Inti now wears a flannel shirt.

              INTI
I propose the following. Why don't you tell us how this whole time travel thing started?

Elena looks up.

              ELENA
You think I'm crazy...

              INTI
I only propose that we take a journey into your story, just as you mentioned before. Perhaps we can better understand your past and with that in mind, help you with your present and future?

              ELENA
Isn't there anything I can do to change your mind, Inti?

              INTI
Please. Let's go back to the beginning and let me get to know you a little bit more.

Elena agrees with a shake of her head.

              ELENA
First, let me get to know you a little better...

Inti smiles kindly, takes a sip of his wine.

              INTI
Go ahead.

              ELENA
What do you dream about at night?

              INTI
I dream of finding the truth...

              ELENA
I'm serious. What are your dreams, what do you expect from life?

              INTI
I will tell you, but then you must answer my question...

> ELENA
> I promise.

> INTI
> The truth is that I dream of everything staying more or less the same. I have a wonderful wife. We have been together for almost 6 years, a year married, a beautiful dog and now the fourth member of the family is on the way. Maybe it's too cheesy, sappy or however you want to classify it. But I only dream that we will be very happy together, for the rest of our lives.

Elena gets emotional, takes her time to speak and keeps her promise. She takes a deep breath.

> ELENA
> When I was a little girl, from a very young age, I used to watch and read everything that had to do with time travel. As old as it was; I saw and read everything. Of course, only fiction. It never occurred to me to investigate how time travel might actually work. Anyway, I think it's something that in one way or another has always been in my life.

Inti looks at her carefully.

> INTI
> Like many children, I imagine.

> ELENA
> And with that, some dreams came to me that, to a large extent, incited what would later lead me to the real possibility of time traveling... It seems that everything is connected and adds up in just the right measure.

> INTI
> What dreams?

Music is heard from the studio to give the right atmosphere to the moment and the light becomes dimmer, leaving Elena at the center of attention, very theatrically.

                    INTI
          Delight us, please.

Elena gets a little nervous again. All the attention is on her. She takes a deep breath before continuing and holds her cane steady.

                    ELENA
          I lived my entire childhood in the
          countryside, on a piece of land in
          the middle of nowhere. And my room
          was pretty much the entire second
          floor... I remember I never had
          curtains; I don't really know
          why... If anything, I never minded.
          The view was beautiful, it looked
          out over the whole field: the fruit
          trees, the hills... Everything and
          nothing at the same time. It really
          was an exceptional sight...
          Sometimes I would go up to the roof
          just to relax with the fresh air
          and the landscape, without even
          imagining how much I would miss
          that place, that view and that air.

Elena is engrossed in telling her story. Inti is very attentive. Elena's eyes shine like never before and her hands very expressively represent each of the spaces she talks about.

As Elena speaks, Inti moves closer and closer to her.

                    ELENA
          In my closet... one of those big,
          long ones you can walk in. That
          closet opened directly into the
          crawl space of the roof of the
          house. All my belongings were
          there, but also, it was a closet
          that my stepparents used to store
          clothes from other seasons and
          things that simply had to be saved
          for some reason that no one really
          understood. It was a very large
          closet full of treasures of all
          kinds.

Elena pauses and notices that Inti is very focused. She smiles gratefully. As Inti gets closer, she starts to speak more quietly. They are in a more intimate setting. The dim lighting accompanies them.

> ELENA
> Right behind those old-fashioned
> clothes that hung at the back of
> the closet because no one ever wore
> them, there was a door that led to
> the crawl space. A place I entered
> many times in my childhood,
> inventing games of all kinds... It
> was kind of a secret place for me.
> Although, of course, everyone knew
> it existed because I also went in
> with my siblings, cousins, and
> friends whenever we could.

A LONG-HAIRED PRODUCTION ASSISTANT comes in to refill the wine glasses. They both sit up and wait for him to leave. Elena takes a sip of wine, eats some nuts and they approach each other again talking very closely and in a low voice.

> ELENA
> The point is that in one of my
> dreams, that door was transformed
> into a portal through which I could
> travel anywhere in the world and at
> any time in history, past or
> future.

Inti opens his eyes in excitement. He is totally enchanted by Elena's dream.

> INTI
> I almost never dream...

> ELENA
> One day I decided to use the portal
> and I appeared in a marketplace in
> China. I'm not sure about the year,
> but there were alleys full of
> people who didn't speak a smidge of
> English.

Elena's wrinkled hands begin to tremble. She covers one with the other and they calm down.

> ELENA
> It was an incredible experience,
> exciting and very... unique...
> Until I wanted to go home.

> INTI
> Why?

                    ELENA
          At some point I realized that I
          couldn't control where I would go
          or what year I would appear in.

                    INTI
          So how did you get back?

                    ELENA
          Every time I crossed the threshold
          I appeared in some year and city
          far from my present, my home and my
          family. And I was just a child.

                    INTI
          Must be intense to lose control so
          much, right? How distressing...

                    ELENA
          After trying as many times as I
          could, I finally showed up in
          Valparaiso, only about 10 years in
          the future... And I decided to give
          up... and take a bus home.

                    INTI
          But you weren't in your time, you
          were in the future...

They both take a drink and sit up. Inti sits back down
properly, and Elena begins to speak louder, as for everyone
to hear.

                    ELENA
          I knew it, but I couldn't keep
          risking the possibility of never
          making it. The possibilities were
          endless. In order to appear in a
          time similar to the one we were
          living in, I could try for a
          lifetime and still not succeed.

Elena takes a swig of wine.

                    ELENA
          When I finally got home, my whole
          family came out to greet me.
          Everyone was very excited.

                    INTI
          I imagine. With good reason.

ELENA
My stepparents were older, my older brother was already an adult, and my little sister, who was a little girl when I left, had now grown up and was bigger than me.

INTI
And what happened?

ELENA
I hugged them all, with a unique satisfaction. I remember it so intensely... But they hugged me tighter... To them, I had been gone for ten years.

Elena gets emotional. Her hands begin to tremble, so she puts one on top of the other to hide her nerves.

ELENA
My stepmother grabbed me by the face, looked at me for a long time, and told me that I hadn't changed a bit since I had disappeared, that I still looked the same.

Elena laughs excitedly. Inti follows her.

INTI
And how did that help you discover this supposed time travel?

ELENA
While it was a dream and nothing more, I'd say it helped me prepare, even question the potential impact of time travel, and consider all the variables.

INTI
And the watch? I thought it had something to do with all this.

ELENA
Let's go back to YOUR dreams, Inti...

INTI
But you asked me about personal dreams and then you told me about actual dreams...

ELENA
In my case, they go hand in hand.

INTI
How so?

ELENA
It's my turn.

INTI
Go ahead.

ELENA
What would you be willing to do to fulfill your dream of a beautiful happy family?

INTI
I think the same thing any parent would do.

ELENA
Any GOOD PARENT. Not just any parent.

Inti smiles gratefully.

INTI
I don't know specifically what you want me to say. Sometimes, it seems like you're pushing me to a specific answer...

ELENA
I'm sorry, I just want to get to know you a little more.

INTI
I would be willing to do anything for my family. In a good way. And I wish I could teach my son all the values that my parents taught me.

ELENA
The value of truth, for example?

Inti laughs.

INTI
Of course.

ELENA
Do you consider yourself a good father?

INTI
I don't know yet.

ELENA
TRUE. But are you prepared?

INTI
As much as I think I can be. More
nervous than prepared, but enough
to do everything in my power to
make sure he doesn't need anything.
And to dedicate myself day by day
to him and my whole family.

Elena smiles at him and takes a sip of her wine, satisfied.

ELENA
The watch came in another dream,
when I was a teenager...

INTI
In another dream? Don't you think
that's too lucky? There are
literally millions of scientists in
the world trying to decipher time
travel and here you are dreaming
all your answers in your sleep.
Well, I don't know if it's
millions, but there must be a lot.

ELENA
It's not that I dream the answers,
I just dreamed up important
questions that somehow helped me
make certain decisions.

Elena takes a deep breath to continue.

ELENA
I was 15 years old maybe... The
dream began with me and a watch to
travel back in time.

They both approach each other again to talk more intimately.

INTI
Like yours.

>   ELENA
>   Similar. When I decided to use it
>   for the first time I went to the
>   past, to an indeterminate time
>   where everything was in black and
>   white, like those really old
>   movies.

Elena begins to explain the dream with the items on the cheese and nut board. She pulls apart a cheese and moves it across the board, indicating that that cheese is her in the story.

>   ELENA
>   When I got to that cinematic past,
>   I immediately encountered a pack of
>   dogs who saw me and attacked me.

She separates five nuts, which "chase" Elena's cheese.

>   ELENA
>   As I escaped, I jumped over the
>   fence of a chicken coop, where I
>   ended up surrounded by the wild
>   dogs, who could see me but not
>   approach... I don't remember if it
>   was because of the fall from that
>   jump, but I remember very clearly
>   that the watch broke irreparably.

Inti moves a little closer to her. Elena makes a separation to indicate the fence that separates her cheese from the pack of nuts.

>   INTI
>   You couldn't go back? Like in the
>   other dream and how you say is
>   happening to you now? Almost
>   foreboding...

Inti smiles sarcastically. Elena realizes that something similar is happening to her.

>   ELENA
>   I couldn't go back. I was stuck in
>   that past forever. I was alone, in
>   a totally indeterminate place in
>   the world and in history, forever.

More nuts surround Elena's cheese, until there are no spaces left to cover, and the cheese is completely enclosed. They both take a swig from their respective glasses.

                    INTI
          And in black and white.

They both laugh. They part again to talk more openly, and
Elena eats her cheese.

                    INTI
          And the watch. The real thing. How
          does it supposedly work?

                    ELENA
          Stop saying "supposedly", please.
          It's clear to everyone that you
          don't believe a word I say.

Inti fills both glasses almost to the brim. Elena watches him
without saying anything.

                    ELENA
          Actually, this is something I don't
          want to explain.

                    INTI
          I can't believe it! We've come this
          far and you don't want to get into
          the most important thing... How
          convenient! This might be what
          would explain it all!

Inti gets up, angry. Elena follows him and takes her drink.

                    ELENA
          It's for everyone's convenience.

                    INTI
          Nothing more and nothing less than
          for everyone's convenience! All of
          this here exclusively at Atalaya!

Inti takes a swig of wine. Elena stares at him for a few
seconds without saying anything, until she surrenders to
emotion, almost on the verge of tears.

She looks at Inti with her teary eyes and then lowers her
gaze as if to prevent him from seeing her so sad.

                    ELENA
               (whispering)
          You're not helping me, Inti. You
          said you were going to help me.

11 **INT. TIMELESS ROOM - DAY** 11

    OVERLAPPING TEXT: Name: Don Eulalio, Age: 80 years, Year: 1958.

    An ELEGANT HUASO (Chilean COWBOY) arrives with an impeccably white jacket, spurs and a perfectly well-kept hat. He has a cleft palate. He takes off his hat and sits down on the couch a little awkwardly.

    He has a small notebook in which he writes with an elegant pen.

    He looks at the record player and listens to Mozart, "Adagio in E Major," not saying anything for a long time.

    On the side table, there is a small inkwell, the one he uses for his pen. He writes a little more in his notebook and looks at the camera again, as if surprised that they are still recording. He stops.

> ELEGANT HUASO
> If there were a possibility of time travel, don't you think we would already know about it?

    He's going to keep writing, but he stops himself.

> ELEGANT HUASO
> When I was about 12 years old, my friend Casimiro and I won our first championship... In the cowboy club of Olmué I think it was.

    He thinks for a few seconds.

> ELEGANT HUASO
> And after that, we were one point from the national championship six times and we won a couple of times. We were formidable.

    He fixes his jacket and smiles.

> ELEGANT HUASO
> I now manage more than ten thousand hectares and have seven children.

    He drinks water from a glass on one of the side tables.

> ELEGANT HUASO
> If I had to go back in time, I wouldn't change a thing.

>   I'd just like to go back to running
>   and riding together one more time
>   with Don Casimiro. Wow, how I miss
>   my friend! Such a brute...

They talk to him behind the scenes.

>   ELEGANT HUASO
>   If I had to go to the future, I
>   would only travel out of curiosity.
>   To see the families that my
>   children will have formed, to meet
>   their children and their children.
>   Sure, I could wait, but why risk
>   it? If I had to go to the future,
>   of course I would allow myself to
>   do that. What else could matter so
>   much?

12 INT. TV SET, TALK-SHOW ATALAYA - NIGHT   12

Inti returns to pick up his glass of wine and now follows Elena to the armchair area.

The armchairs have changed and are now blue. Elena sits down. Inti approaches her and, squatting, takes her hands. Elena looks at him suspiciously.

>   INTI
>   I'm sorry if I've been too harsh,
>   but to seek the truth, "to eat and
>   to drink is the very least".

Elena smiles.

>   INTI
>   If we seek the truth, we must
>   confront it whatever it may be.
>
>   ELENA
>   Whether we like it or not.
>
>   INTI
>   Whether we or you like it.

Elena and Inti smile together.

>   ELENA
>   Everything I've said is true, Inti.

                    INTI
          We are no longer seeking the truth
          for the people in their homes, or
          for me, but also for you. Do you
          understand me, Mrs. Elena?

Elena doesn't answer.

                    ELENA
          Can you imagine what would happen
          if everyone could have access to a
          time machine?

                    INTI
          Yeah right! It wouldn't be
          EVERYONE, clearly.

                    ELENA
          Even worse. Who would use it and
          for what purposes? The elites, the
          politicians, big businessmen,
          celebrities, the world powers? With
          everything I've been through, I
          can't even imagine what a time
          travel war would be like.

Inti stands up and sits down in his armchair.

                    INTI
          I honestly don't see the logic in
          it. You come on a TV show to
          SUPPOSEDLY travel in time on
          camera, pretending to change
          history, but you say it's
          irresponsible to explain how. If
          people really saw time travel on
          television, don't you think that at
          least someone would be able to
          investigate and come to the same
          conclusions that you SUPPOSEDLY did
          to mimic time travel? Let's stop
          kidding around, please. Wouldn't
          that be equally irresponsible?

Elena doesn't answer.

                    INTI
          I don't understand you, Mrs. Elena.
          I can't agree with you at all, I'm
          sorry.

                    ELENA
          How could you agree with something
          you don't understand?

INTI
Mrs. Elena, you've seen this show before, haven't you?

ELENA
No. I'm sorry.

INTI
What? But did you at least know of it?

ELENA
Very little actually. Almost nothing, to be honest.

INTI
I can't believe it. Why then did you come if you hadn't even seen us once?

Elena smiles politely.

ELENA
(with embarrassment)
I told you, Inti. I come from the future to save you and change my history.

INTI
Of course, to save me. If you really believe that, then give me something else. How are we going to convince all the families at home that time travel is possible and a reality?

ELENA
Shall I tell you about the twin towers?

INTI
What about the towers...?

ELENA
Should I tell you that flying cars won't arrive for a very long time, long after the arrival of the new millennium? That they will finally find Paul Schäfer?... Although none of those things will be able to be verified in the short term. What can I tell you that completely convinces you?

INTI
Very complex, really.

ELENA
And you, who likes soccer, what if I tell you that Chile lost in the round of 16 to Brazil 4-1 in the World Cup, but that we won two of the World Cups between the new 40's and 50's?

INTI
I wish we got to play against Brazil, because for that we would have to beat Italy first!

Elena smiles.

ELENA
Or tie.

INTI
But it clearly won't be as you say. 4-1 is a tremendous gamble.

ELENA
As the DNA test has already made clear, nothing I say about the future will be enough.

INTI
Of course not. And even if everything you say were to happen, how could it be proof enough that you come from the future? We've had guests who say they have certain premonitions, but that doesn't make them time travelers... They could very well be good calculators of the future playing the odds, right?

ELENA
Nothing I say will ever be enough. Never.

INTI
Without concrete evidence, arguments are just words... So, I can't help but think that you didn't come prepared enough? Curious, to say the least.

ELENA
Of course, I came prepared. My watch was supposed to suffice, and that I wouldn't be here trying to make it work for so long.

Elena looks at her watch again.

INTI
OK. You can't or won't explain how it technically works. At least you will be able to tell us HOW you came to create a watch capable of time travel, being only a psychologist and a teacher...

ELENA
"Only" a psychologist and teacher? Do you think that with my 90 years you can define me only as a psychologist and teacher?

INTI
You know what I mean...

ELENA
No, I have no idea what you mean...

INTI
You are very different from what any of us could imagine for someone who invents a way to travel through time.

ELENA
Sometimes I forget that there is still a long way to go here.

INTI
You know...

ELENA
What I can say is that time travel is a discovery rather than an invention. And it seems only reasonable to me that it should come from someone who does not belong to the context in which a discovery of this kind is expected to occur.

INTI
How so? Why?

ELENA
When science and technology spend years arguing about whether or not something could happen, other people are looking for ways to make things happen... And there are other people, like me, who find themselves with answers to questions that we have barely been able to ask ourselves.

Maybe it's because I'm ONLY a psychologist and a teacher that the answers came... Maybe it's because I don't have the same paradigms and limitations in THINKING that I understand so much of what others are looking for in such a biased way.

INTI
Like those intelligence games that if you don't solve immediately, are almost impossible to solve later.

ELENA
Precisely.

INTI
Paradigms...

ELENA
Paradigms.

Silence.

INTI
So, we don't have anything. It's pointless, isn't it? Because words are not enough, no matter how eloquent they may be. "Easier said than done."

ELENA
Of course. Whatever I say, you will continue to be immersed in a paradigm that has been established since the beginning of humanity.

INTI
Again with same thing! What paradigm?

ELENA
The past cannot be changed.

INTI
But you say that now you can.

                    ELENA
          Of course, because I discovered it
          by mistake. Probably, if it hadn't
          been for the mistake, I would never
          have discovered it. And it's surely
          for the same reason that no one has
          done it before. Such a paradigm is
          so strong that you may have the
          solution in front of you and you
          will not be able to see it, let
          alone accept it.

                    INTI
          I don't think so.

                    ELENA
          Let's see, can I trust you?

                    INTI
          We may have our differences, but of
          course you can trust me.

Elena takes off her watch, makes some adjustments that take a
few seconds, and hands it to Inti.

                    ELENA
          Take it. You can't check it , but
          you can try using it yourself. Just
          press the button and you're off.
          You'll be in my time for a minute
          and then you'll be back on the
          show.

Inti opens his eyes.

                    INTI
          Is it that easy? And will I be in
          the future?

                    ELENA
          If it works for you, it's that
          easy.

Inti stares at the clock, as if looking for the trap.

                    INTI
          But it doesn't even work!

                    ELENA
          But you can give it a try... If it
          doesn't work, this will be just
          another anecdote for your show.

Inti laughs, nervous. Look behind the scenes to find out what to do.

                        ELENA
            Let's go. Put the watch on and
            listen to me.

Elena takes a swig of wine. Inti smiles and hands her the watch back. Elena receives it and puts it back on immediately, making it clear that there won't be another chance.

                        ELENA
            That's just my point.

                        INTI
            You came to this show so that we
            could test you, not me.

                        ELENA
            You had the solution in your hands.
            The answer to your precious truth.
            I pressured you to use it and you
            still were incapable of seeing
            beyond your paradigms. That's my
            point. Your beliefs, your ignorance
            and fears completely paralyzed you.
            Do I still have to say something
            that might convince you that time
            travel is possible?

Elena makes a few new adjustments to her watch.

                        INTI
            What do you propose?

                        ELENA
            The only way to prove it is by
            traveling here live and during the
            show.

                        INTI
            Easy to say.

                        ELENA
            Therefore, for my sake and for your
            precious truth, I must find a
            solution and get the watch working
            again.

                        INTI
            OK, but if we could find a
            solution...

You seem too calm to be taking into
account that some of the risks are
disappearing from history,
collapsing the universe, exploding,
or who knows what else.

              ELENA
What makes you think that those are
the risks?

              INTI
It's what we've always seen...

Elena smiles.

              ELENA
I'm more afraid of the last part.

Inti laughs complicitly. They again achieve a certain harmony in the conversation.

              INTI
Of collapsing the universe or of
exploding?

              ELENA
No. Of everything else. I'm afraid
of that which we don't even
consider a possibility.

              INTI
Fear of the unknown? To be wrong?

              ELENA
To be wrong, of course. I can't be
sure how time works; all its
possibilities. Mostly because
despite having read or researched,
I'm just a former teacher and
psychologist who figured out how to
travel. By mistake. And as much as
you think you know, no one else has
actually done it EVER before. There
are only theories, all different
and with a high probability of
error.

              INTI
So then? What are you most afraid
of? To be wrong or just to be
crazy?

ELENA
I'm afraid of not being crazy. Of traveling back in time and making changes that drive me crazy. Or being able to travel back in time and remember two completely different lives as a result of the changes I made... or not being able to make the changes I really want. That somehow everything that has already happened to me in my own history, and the world's, are inevitable events.

INTI
But you still would have decided to travel.

ELENA
Somehow, I think that as Blanca Goycoolea said: "with human beings, curiosity has always overcome common sense". And honestly, I can't afford to delay any longer... If it doesn't work out, it would be a great sadness..., but if it does, it would be... Really incredible. A true new life.

Inti checks one of his memory aid cards.

INTI
Another thing that strikes me is that I see that you really know very little about how time works. If it were possible, how could you dare to think of changing history, if you don't even know enough?

ELENA
I think I know enough for someone who will be taking all the risks. Everyone thinks that the younger ones are the ones who should take the most risks, but they don't realize that it is the older ones who have nothing to lose. And therefore, those who have the responsibility to take the risks that can change and improve the world. Let that be our legacy.

> INTI
> It all sounds very convenient and at the same time perhaps very convincing. The gift of gab.

> ELENA
> I was a teacher for a long time, sorry.

> INTI
> However, it's a legacy you don't want to share.

> ELENA
> No, not yet. No.

13 INT. TIMELESS ROOM - DAY 13

OVERLAY TEXT: Name: Lucrecio, Age: 60 years, Year: 1940.

A CORPULENT PAINTER is dressed in blue overalls while sitting in the same vintage armchair, facing the camera. He has a cleft palate.

Mozart is still heard, "Vesperae solennes de confessore" this time.

He has white paint on his clothes, hair, face, and hands. He has a metal lunch box on top of him and eats a meat empanada.

> CORPULENT PAINTER
> First of all, if I didn't know anything about time travel, it would never occur to me to travel. It would be like handing a car to a little kid. And do you know how much a car costs, and how would a little kid drive it?

He eats a little and continues speaking with his mouth full.

> CORPULENT PAINTER
> Of course. How am I going to put myself at risk with something I don't know how to handle?

He keeps eating while he thinks for a few more seconds.

> CORPULENT PAINTER
> It sounds interesting, but we don't know enough about it to be willing to take risks and then leave our families stranded.

He wipes his mouth with a napkin.

> CORPULENT PAINTER
> Some will say that they would come back to save their families from the earthquake and others would certainly do something about the war. But I don't. I would rather focus on my family... and on working. As things are, we must be thankful that at least some of us still have jobs. One day at a time is how you move ahead, not with a time machine... Sure, we will always have problems and we have to learn to live with them.

He wipes himself with the napkin, puts it away, and reaches for his empanada, until he stops mid-bite to speak again.

> CORPULENT PAINTER
> "Let bygones be bygones," as they say.

He laughs and continues to eat his empanada.

14 INT. TV SET, TALK-SHOW ATALAYA - NIGHT   14

Inti and Elena continue talking. On the table you can see all the wine bottles they have drunk. All with a blue label.

A PRODUCTION ASSISTANT with a ponytail arrives and takes them away. Elena gives him the glass so that he can pour her a little more.

> ELENA
> To give you a little more understanding, I wish you would answer the question you owe me.

> INTI
> What question?

> ELENA
> Where would you go and why? What would you do if it was the only time travel you could do? You can go to the past, to the future, whenever you want. Round trip, of course.

> INTI
> It depends ...

ELENA
Of course it depends, that's the difficulty...

INTI
To the past, perhaps?

ELENA
To look at your past life or a historical past? To destroy Hitler, for example? Putin?

INTI
Putin?

Inti frowns.

ELENA
Right...

INTI
If I go and make Hitler disappear before anything he did... As good as that sounds for the future, we don't really know how that would affect... the world.

ELENA
Nor you.

INTI
How do you mean?

ELENA
That you wouldn't know how it would affect you either. To your personal life, to your family, or to your very own existence.

INTI
Of course. And on the one hand, you would also have to be able to kill someone. Even if it is Hitler, I would have to "stop" him long before he comes to power. That moment would be the new "here and now", so I'd really have to dare...

ELENA
When he had not yet committed any atrocities.

> INTI
> Of course. And on the other hand, Hitler was also a figure who partly emerged as a result of many things and a certain historical context that goes beyond his own figure, right?

Inti takes a long drink of water.

> INTI
> I don't want to be misunderstood. Of course what I mean is that it sounds tempting as a perfect answer to the question...

> ELENA
> But...

> INTI
> But... we don't know what would happen if we got rid of Hitler. Would another Hitler appear in his place? One that's even worse? That would leave an even bigger mess? More than the original Hitler left behind?...

> INTI
> It's just that it's a single trip... You really have to think about it... I don't know, I'm not sure.

> ELENA
> Of course you're not sure, and why?

> INTI
> Because there are so many variables... It also depends on the theory of time we believe in.

> ELENA
> Aha!

Elena gets excited. That's what she wanted to hear.

> ELENA
> Of course. It depends on the theory of time THAT IT IS REAL, not the one we believe in. If you don't know the consequences of a change in time, how can you make such a decision?

And how do you make sure it doesn't affect your personal life?

                    INTI
You can't.

                    ELENA
But still, without being clear about how time works... wouldn't you try to make some changes in your personal or family history? Maybe save a life? Tell someone who has died of cancer to get a preventive exam well before their death to prevent it from happening?

Silence. Inti looks at her suspiciously. Elena insists.

                    INTI
Yes, it may be that in the end the most reasonable option is to make a smaller change and leave Hitler for a possible second chance. Maybe start with change related to something more personal, something more controlled and predictable.

                    ELENA
Perfect.

Elena smiles with satisfaction.

                    INTI
Perfect what?

                    ELENA
You've just demonstrated an important uncertainty.

                    INTI
How can I not hesitate? Besides, I'm just playing along.

                    ELENA
I pressed you with a hypothetical story and you are already weighing humanity on one hand, and your life and personal interests on the other.

                    INTI
But it's hypothetical, we're not talking about a real scenario.

ELENA
Precisely! If with such a short and hypothetical conversation you are already thinking about putting your own personal interests above those of humanity, imagine the decision you would be able to make if you really had that unique opportunity to travel back in time.

INTI
If the possibility were real, of course I'd think about it a little more... Is that why you think no one else should be able to travel back in time?

Elena takes a sip from her glass of wine. Inti insists.

INTI
What hypocrisy! Why do you think YOU have the right to change history?

ELENA
I don't think I have the right to do it over anyone else, not at all, but at least I'm the only one who's figured out a way to travel in time.

Inti smiles. He accepts defeat but knows that it is only theoretical.

INTI
OK, OK. But we lack substantiation. Practical evidence.

ELENA
The first testimony for everything is words.

INTI
And action.

ELENA
Of course...

INTI
Mrs. Elena..., let's get on with your exercise... You, who are supposed to have figured out how to travel through time...

Elena interrupts him.

> ELENA
> You seem to have a hard time even pretending that you believe anything I say. Even if it's just in the slightest.

> INTI
> You are having a hard time convincing me that it's true.

They both smile, complicit. Elena doesn't let him continue with the question.

> ELENA
> The first thing is to understand that for a first trip, the possibilities are too many.

> INTI
> Sure, but...

> ELENA
> Not only in choosing a historical or personal moment to travel to, but also the consequences that any time expedition can have.

> INTI
> Of course...

> ELENA
> In the end, there are several questions: Which theory of time is the real one? How does my trip affect my personal story? How will my trip affect the world around me?

> INTI
> OK, but the evidence.

> ELENA
> I'm sorry, I haven't talked to anyone about this...

> INTI
> Really? With no one? Don't you have a friend, a pal out there that you can talk to about these things?

Elena doesn't answer.

INTI
Really? No one?

ELENA
No. And I didn't intend to talk to you about it either, but something happened to the watch.

INTI
Why haven't you talked about it with anyone else? Maybe that could have helped you somewhat.

ELENA
Because others would have asked me the same questions I had already asked myself. Or worse, they'd look at me like you do...

INTI
Do you say it because you're a woman or because of your age?

ELENA
I meant because of the supposed impossibility of time travel.

INTI
Of course, I don't think you can't travel back in time because you're a woman or because of your age.

ELENA
Of course.

INTI
And to be clear, I'm not looking at you in any particular way.

ELENA
I'm talking about that look of disbelief. That I'm definitely crazy so it's not worth listening to my reasons.

She takes a long swig of wine. She thinks about it a bit and checks the time again. Inti notices the gesture and looks at the time on his own watch as well.

INTI
But what are the chances then?

ELENA
I think, because I'm neither a scientist nor an expert...

INTI
Of course, because supposedly this is your first trip.

ELENA
I believe that time can't just be linear.

INTI
OK. So how would you describe it?

ELENA
Let's see. Yes, one possibility is that time is linear and everything I do in the past affects the future.

INTI
Very movie-like... But it makes sense, right? Simplicity is appealing.

ELENA
But if time is one and linear, when I travel to the past and influence the timeline, there is the possibility of generating a paradox.

INTI
One that would have catastrophic consequences? Like the universe exploding, or something?

ELENA
I do not know. I think that anything can be. The truth is that I didn't want to complicate myself with things that were so difficult to understand... Because if I really go back to the past and create a paradox, and as a result me or the whole world disappear, wouldn't that be a paradox in itself?

Inti doesn't know what to say.

ELENA
Never mind. I suppose maybe that could be a possibility. Although I can't understand why the universe would allow something like that to happen.

INTI
You speak of the universe as if it were a living entity.

ELENA
Sometimes I believe it is...

INTI
But there are more possibilities...

ELENA
I suppose so. Another possibility would be that every time I travel back in time and generate a change, the timeline splits in two. Therefore, if I travel to the past and make a change, when I travel back to the future, I would be entering another timeline different from the one I came from.

INTI
How problematic...

ELENA
I would have a different life and different memories than everyone else had from that point on.

INTI
I don't know if that was enough clarification.

ELENA
It becomes madness.

INTI
I assume you don't believe in that, then?

ELENA
I think time is simpler than that. Although I don't know if "simple" is the right word... There is another theory that says that time settles itself, automatically.

> It's still linear, but the moment you travel back in time, everything falls back into place. You could make alterations, but you wouldn't remember them, because everything has accommodated to make it so.

Elena reaches into her pocket and pulls out a small ball of purple yarn.

> **ELENA**
> Time, for me, is like a ball of yarn. But with no beginning or end, all intertwined and connected in different places. But alive, changing and in permanent motion.

The ball of yarn is confusing, you can't see where it begins or ends and it's clearly impossible to follow the path of the cord without getting lost in all the twists and turns it takes to be a proper ball of yarn.

Elena gently runs one of her fingers through the yarn, as if following the cord in one of its fractions.

> **ELENA**
> Perhaps, time is a paradox in itself. I think time settles down and everything happens as it should at the same time. There isn't much to do. Moreover, energy is neither created nor destroyed, it is only transformed...

Elena is engrossed. She stands up and starts walking from side to side without looking at Inti.

> **ELENA**
> You know that you are a consequence of the choices you've made, the upbringing you had, the relationships you've shared, and finally the context in which you have lived.

> **INTI**
> I guess...

> **ELENA**
> Basically, you are the result of a perfect mix of variables that make you who you are now.

INTI
Let's just say I get it.

Elena smiles. She looks at Inti.

ELENA
So, if you're the result of everything that went on before, do you think you're really making decisions of your own? Or are they just based on that history, and are the consequence of all that happened before?

INTI
So, there is no real freedom of choice, no free will?

ELENA
Just that. There is no such thing as free will. We are not free to choose!

INTI
I don't think so. I think there has to be a part that is really our own decision.

Elena continues to walk in front of Inti who watches her carefully.

ELENA
On what basis do you say that?

INTI
That at some point I can choose freely?

ELENA
"We are here precisely in search of something a little more concrete than faith."

INTI
If there is no free will, there is nothing.

ELENA
If there is no free will and if everything is somehow written down... We are truly, absolutely free.

INTI
That doesn't make sense.

ELENA
If everything is written in a language that no one can read or in a book that no one can find, how does it affect me if it is all written? If I don't know if life is worth my effort or not... I just have to push myself. Of course, if that kind of effort is something that's already defined for me.

INTI
OK, but what does free will have to do with all this time travel stuff?

ELENA
Everything.

Elena takes a drink of her wine.

ELENA
If you take into account that everything is written, I doubt that there is a way for new timelines to be generated when making changes to this one... Also, you can consider that, ultimately, the changes you make to the timeline are just something else that is meant to happen.

INTI
I don't understand... Are you trying to justify yourself by the possible effects that changing history could have?

ELENA
Fate is inevitable, but we don't know it, and that includes the possible changes from time traveling.

INTI
It's depressing.

                    ELENA
          How can it be depressing?! If
          everything is written and being
          written at the same time, if
          everything is permanently falling
          into place, we would simply forget
          that we made changes and continue
          to make them as long as it is
          written that we should make them.
          For example, we might permanently
          seek to be better people or just
          save my father, save you.

                    INTI
          Or make us win the World Cup!

Elena falls silent.

                    INTI
          Sure, if I could really travel back
          in time.

Elena is upset and doesn't know how to continue. She sits
down again.

                    INTI
          Of course, whatever is in your own
          interest. If so, you could change
          the timeline until you have a
          perfect life, right? And all the
          other consequences, for better or
          worse, you just wouldn't know or
          remember that it was you yourself
          who caused them. And so, you would
          avoid responsibility and remorse...

                    ELENA
          If it's written, I wouldn't be the
          one to cause it...

                    INTI
          So, assuming that you were really a
          time traveler and that you
          fervently believe in that... Are
          you willing to come into this time
          and this show, make changes and
          affect the timeline and history;
          and also, say it all on camera,
          without thinking about the
          consequences?

Silence.

                    INTI
          Of course, I understand and thank
          your intention and effort in
          wanting to save me.

Elena takes another sip of wine.

                    ELENA
          It was serendipity, finding a way
          to travel back in time. I wasn't
          looking for it... It was clearly
          written... And, of course, I think
          about the consequences. The
          difference is that after... I think
          I just wouldn't think about them
          anymore...

Silence.

                    ELENA
          What would YOU do if you were in my
          shoes?

                    INTI
          It's the same justification a
          psychopathic killer might have for
          committing his heinous acts: "If I
          did it, it's only because I had to.
          It was my destiny."

15 **INT. TIMELESS ROOM - DAY**   15

OVERLAY TEXT: Name: Sara, Age: 25, Year: Undetermined.

A WOMAN WITH AN AFRO is sitting on the couch.

On the record player, we continue with Mozart (Fantasia in D Minor).

The woman is dressed in a tight, yellow jumpsuit. The suit has a high collar and covers her entire body. She is wearing long blue rubber gloves, also tight-fitting. On her head she has a kind of transparent fishbowl-like helmet, totally sealed with the collar of the suit.

Through the helmet you can see that the woman has a cleft palate.

Her long boots, also made of rubber and blue, once again highlight how protected she is. On her arm she carries a rubber purse, from which she takes out a small copper bottle. With a couple of drops from the bottle, she "cleans her hands" with gloves on.

She's clearly from a future where something serious happened and everyone is already used to being absolutely protected.

She's sad and nervous about the camera.

> **WOMAN WITH AFRO**
> If I could travel back in time just once... phew... It's a very difficult question... I do not know... Although the issue of radiation is very obvious, I don't know if that's what motivates me the most.

She looks at her gloves.

> **WOMAN WITH AFRO**
> It's just that it seems to be inevitable. Although it is difficult to imagine, there will always be incompetent people, with power, capable of harming the whole world, bombing everything, regardless of whether they are from protected sectors or a danger to themselves...

She's still nervously looking at her blue gloves.

> **WOMAN WITH AFRO**
> Whatever we do to avoid that, there will always be people like this, and NOTHING ensures that it will be the last time it happens... That's why, I suppose, if I could travel back in time just once, I would take the opportunity to connect with something more personal, more intimate.

The woman looks up and gets excited.

She takes a deep breath.

> **WOMAN WITH AFRO**
> I'm sure I'd go to my mom, back to that time when I was very young... To tell her that despite everything she was going through... with me, at that time... Single...

She looks behind the scenes.

                        WOMAN WITH AFRO
                  May I?

She waits a few seconds.

                        WOMAN WITH AFRO
                  Are you sure?

She takes a deep breath, saves the air in her lungs and
slowly takes off the helmet, leaving it next to her on the
couch. She gathers strength and allows herself to breathe
little by little.

Suddenly, she is surprised and excited.

                        WOMAN WITH AFRO
                  I can't believe it...

She breathes nervously for a few seconds, until she finally
accepts that the air is healthy. A tear runs down her cheek.

                        WOMAN WITH AFRO
                  I just can't believe it...

She cleans her face and takes a deep breath before
continuing.

                        WOMAN WITH AFRO
                  I'm sorry, I'm sorry. I just can't
                  believe it... Thanks a lot...
                  Really, thank you so much...

She takes a few seconds to calm down, looks at her hands
again and takes another breath to continue.

                        WOMAN WITH AFRO
                  The first thing I would do is go
                  back in time to see my mom... I'd
                  just like to tell her that
                  everything is going to be okay.

Pause.

                        WOMAN WITH AFRO
                  I'd come to her door and say, in
                  some way that she can feel it's
                  real, "everything's going to be
                  okay." Despite how lonely she may
                  feel at that moment, with a newborn
                  baby, not knowing how to get ahead,
                  in that world we lived in... I
                  would tell her that... And I'd hold
                  her tight...

                        And hopefully it would give her
                        some peace of mind for the future.

She wipes away her tears.

                        WOMAN WITH AFRO
                        That's what I'd do if I could
                        travel back in time. I'd tell my
                        mom that everything's going to be
                        okay.

Pause.

                        WOMAN WITH AFRO
                            (whispers)
                        Everything's going to be okay.

16 INT. TV SET, TALK-SHOW ATALAYA - NIGHT   16

Elena is crestfallen, totally devastated by her inability to travel.

                        INTI
                        Mrs. Elena, we are coming to the
                        end of the show, and we have proven
                        that time travel is simply not
                        possible. At least not for now. Not
                        to mention the possibility of you
                        being my daughter.

                        ELENA
                        We haven't demonstrated anything
                        yet.

                        INTI
                        That's exactly what I'm talking
                        about.

                        ELENA
                        I haven't stopped thinking about
                        it... There must definitely be
                        something that isn't allowing me to
                        travel...

Elena looks around, as if looking for an answer.

                        ELENA
                        What am I supposed to do now?

                        INTI
                        Just let it go.

                         ELENA
                    No. Not yet.

Inti takes a deep breath and stands up. He has put on a new
shirt and is wearing a tie.

                         INTI
                    Beyond seeking the truth, I would
                    like to express my concern for your
                    own mental health... With a fixed
                    idea of something that you are no
                    longer able to demonstrate... It's
                    gone from being a bad joke, a while
                    ago, to something worrisome.

                         ELENA
                    It's just that I can still...

                         INTI
                    You can't, Mrs. Elena. You can't do
                    anything. Listen to me, please. You
                    are a psychologist. From a
                    psychological point of view, could
                    you explain this?

Silence.

                         INTI
                    If you still have the fixed idea
                    that you can convince us of its
                    truth, just humour me, just as you
                    asked me to do with you. This is
                    your chance. We can continue for a
                    few more minutes. Only if you
                    decide to help us.

                         ELENA
                    Help you with what?

                         INTI
                    This is the "hypothetical"
                    situation: you don't know about
                    time travel. No one in the world
                    knows about time travel. What would
                    you say to a patient of yours who
                    comes in with a similar story?

                         ELENA
                    I'm not crazy, you know?

Inti doesn't answer.

ELENA
I would tell them to explain themselves to me about their journey. I'd love to know...

INTI
Don't pull my leg, Mrs. Elena, please. Seriously. No one in their right mind would start with that.

ELENA
I understand, but I always start from the premise that they are speaking to me with the truth, even if that truth only applies to themselves.

INTI
But what would you think THE TRUTH is?

ELENA
I don't think it's necessary to explain. Everyone understood your point already.

INTI
Mrs. Elena, at this minute you must know that you are telling us a story that only you believe to be true, but that is not a reality that can be shared with the rest of the world... And that has been proven.

ELENA
If I'm wrong, how would you explain all this?

INTI
How would you explain it, Mrs. Elena? I don't have anything to explain...

ELENA
If I weren't the one saying it... If I can't get any proof of certainty...

INTI
Of course I wouldn't look for it, nor would I find it if I did.

ELENA
If I really don't have a way to believe this person...

Elena stops. She takes a deep breath and continues. It's not easy.

ELENA
It's possible that some major trauma or event triggered something — some kind of defense mechanism, I guess. It's a rather simplistic answer, though. Obviously, I would need to talk to this patient more.

Inti walks, approaches her, and bends down to speak to her more intimately.

INTI
I'm not a psychologist, but the abrupt death of your father, his absence, the search for that figure in your life, do you think maybe that would be enough?

ELENA
It's too complex a story to be making up every detail, don't you think?

INTI
I don't know... Weren't the stories of your patients complex?

ELENA
I could say it's an important piece of information... And that something, at a specific moment in their life, was linked to that traumatic moment. And that ended up acting as a trigger.

INTI
Of course.

ELENA
But I don't know... I wasn't even born when my father died and I don't remember anything about my mother, of course... In addition, a significant percentage of the population has lost one of their parents and they are not inventing these complex lives...

> Why in my case should I have to elaborate something like this, with so many details?

Inti gets up and goes back to his armchair.

> INTI
> Sometimes, a good lie needs a lot of detail to be convincing. Especially if you need to convince the mind of a psychologist.

> ELENA
> But all my memories...

> INTI
> A good lie is made up of pure truths.

Elena doesn't answer.

> INTI
> I don't want to be a brute, but you yourself said that you were not born at the time of your father's death. What if that isn't true? And when it all happened, you were still a child who saw everything that you say traumatized your mother so much; And that trauma was, in fact, more your own?

Elena is bothered by Inti's interpretations. Inti smiles with satisfaction.

> INTI
> You're doubting... Let's go further then. Let us seek the truth.

Inti looks at the camera, at his viewers.

> INTI
> If I understood correctly, the moment that triggered this "story", could have something to do with the trauma of the past. So, let's go to that moment...

> ELENA
> What moment?

                    INTI
          When you figured out how to travel
          in time. That would be the moment,
          right? What was it like?

                    ELENA
          What? No. I can't go into details.

                    INTI
          I don't want the technical
          explanation. I'm not interested at
          this point. Tell me, what were you
          doing? Where and how did it happen?

Elena doesn't answer.

                    INTI
          There's nothing, right? Nothing
          concrete, at least.

                    ELENA
          It's embarrassing. Because we're
          talking from the basis that I'm
          crazy. And of course, everything
          seems to justify it!

                    INTI
          And nothing justifies the real
          possibility of time travel. See?
          Nothing but questionable papers or
          metaphysical ideas, possibilities,
          memories, and supposed unverifiable
          futures...

Elena is silent for a few seconds. She calms down.

                    ELENA
          OK. I'll play along. I disagree. I
          must. But I just think it's fair.

She pours herself a glass of wine and drinks it completely.
Takes a deep breath.

                    INTI
          Perfect.

                    ELENA
          To begin with, I discovered time
          travel by mistake...

                    INTI
          But how?

> ELENA
> I didn't meet... My dad. I didn't know my mom either, and I lost them both because of a madman, and because of being in the wrong place at the wrong time... or the right time to trigger the story of my life. I've always thought, what if that madman hadn't been there?...

Silence.

Elena continues as she points her hands at Inti and describes him:

> ELENA
> The only thing I know about my father is what he did for a living, where he died, and the consequences of his death on my life. And the only thing I have left of him was a watch, which came to me almost 90 years after his death.

> INTI
> So how did the watch come to you?

> ELENA
> Another of the victims' sons.

Elena looks behind the camera, as if looking for the victim. Then she looks at her watch.

> ELENA
> He mistakenly received it as the only object left of his father. His grandson, after all these years, discovered that it hadn't really been his.

> INTI
> How?

> ELENA
> By means of the only record that exists of that show.

> INTI
> Are you referring to this show?

> ELENA
> Yes, THIS show.

                    INTI
          And the madman he's talking about
          would be José, right?

                    ELENA
          The only guest registered, and with
          potentially explosive devices. José
          Mella, yes.

Inti opens his eyes, totally incredulous.

                    INTI
          So, you reported him?

Elena doesn't answer.

                    INTI
          I can't believe it! Of course it
          was you!

Inti stands up, walks back and forth, and sits down again. He
takes a deep breath trying to calm himself down and decides
to continue.

                    INTI
          OK... And this person handed you
          the watch, just like that?

                    ELENA
          He was researching his family. And
          in the photo, many decades later,
          he realized that someone else was
          wearing the watch. As he needed to
          investigate, he contacted me, we
          talked and he gave it to me.

                    INTI
          And did that watch travel back in
          time? Just like that?

Elena doesn't answer.

                    INTI
          TRUE. You don't want to explain any
          of that... And could it be that
          that moment is the trigger we're
          talking about? That link to the
          traumas of your past?

                    ELENA
          Important details are missing, of
          course... Nothing is that simple...

Inti interrupts her.

                    INTI
            You mean this watch, right?

Inti rolls up the sleeves of his shirt to show off his watch.
Elena looks at him carefully and her eyes widen in surprise.

                    ELENA
            That watch, of course!

Elena freezes staring at Inti's watch.

                    INTI
            ¿Mrs. Elena?

Elena snaps out of her trance and throws herself desperately
at Inti. The table falls over, the wine glasses, the lamp,
everything is a mess.

17 **INT. TIMELESS ROOM - DAY**   17

   OVERLAY TEXT: Name: Hilaria, Age: 70 years, Year: 1932.

   On the couch is A LADY WITH APRON from the 30's. She has a
   cleft palate.

   Mozart is still playing (String Quartet N° 19).

                    LADY WITH APRON
            If I could travel back in time, I
            would make the best of it and spend
            more time reading... and well,
            writing, of course... I always
            wanted to write more... Maybe even
            publish a book of short stories...,
            or maybe a novel...

   The lady is silent for a few seconds.

                    LADY WITH APRON
            But in the end, it sounds like more
            work... Since for that, I would
            have to do what I need to do to
            remain myself. And at the same
            time, dedicate time to what I
            want... If so, it's a lot of
            work... And what happens if I don't
            write anymore? do I try a different
            life?

   She looks at the ground, thinking about her answer.

                    LADY WITH APRON
          No, I don't know, actually... I
          think if I could really travel back
          in time just once, I'd visit those
          distant, old uncles I don't know...
          Or I would go to see my
          grandparents when they were young
          and share with them their best
          moments...

She shakes her head.

                    LADY WITH APRON
          No... Actually, I think I would go
          to see my daughters when they were
          little. I know the question refers
          to travelling only once, but if I
          could, I would go many times... at
          that time..., before they had
          studies, a job, a house and a
          family of their own...

The lady looks at the wrinkles in her hands.

                    LADY WITH APRON
          I would go back to take advantage
          of the time with them a little
          more.

18 INT. TV SET, TALK-SHOW ATALAYA - EVENING   18

Elena struggles with Inti to take the watch from him, but he won't allow it.

Inti, who is now wearing a blue suit, turns away from her in fear. He is perplexed and stares at her defensively. Elena pulls herself together and fixes her clothes.

                    ELENA
          I know why it didn't work... I
          know...

Elena pauses to think about what she has just discovered.

                    INTI
          Do you still think you're a time
          traveler?

                    ELENA
          Are you still looking for the
          truth, Inti?

Inti doesn't answer.

> ELENA
> It all makes sense now.

> INTI
> Nothing makes sense right now.

Elena is not listening to him anymore.

> ELENA
> Of course, how could I be so careless?

Inti sees that Elena is very nervous, approaches her little by little and helps her sit down.

> INTI
> Please calm down and sit down.

Elena sits down, slowly.

> ELENA
> I'm so dumb...

> INTI
> It can happen to anyone. Especially with the traumas you have.

> ELENA
> Of course I have traumas... Who doesn't?

Inti shrugs. Elena stands up again and starts walking from side to side. Inti also stops and waits for her in front of her armchair.

> ELENA
> Don't you understand? Just by preventing José from coming, I saved your life...

> INTI
> But why come to the show? Why not just make the report? Clearly there has to be something more. Something psychological, right? Don't you think so? Don't you?

> ELENA
> I just needed to meet you, I told you so!

> INTI
> In case you were wrong, right?

ELENA
You don't understand.

INTI
Explain. It's your last chance.

ELENA
If you're so willing to find the truth above all else, you'd just hand me your watch. Anyway, my work here is already done.

Elena smiles.

INTI
Your mission, of course.

ELENA
All in one trip: I save you, I get to know you, and I travel back again.

INTI
It's that simple. And you get to have the life you want.

Elena is nervous again and her hands are shaking.

INTI
You can't travel, Mrs. Elena, and you're not my daughter. And we ran out of time. Actually, it seems to me that you can go now.

ELENA
And your truth? Will you do nothing? Will you continue in the same paradigm out of ignorance and pride?

Elena takes a few steps, approaching Inti.

INTI
This watch was given to me by my wife when we found out we were going to have a BOY! I would never give it to you!

ELENA
Yes, I can travel! The problem is the watch... It's my watch and your watch... Your watch is ticking, and when I received it, it was destroyed.

                    INTI
          What are you talking about, Mrs.
          Elena? Please stop all this!

Elena gets quite close to Inti and they face each other. She
grabs her cane in both hands and takes a deep breath. She
lowers her head, looking at the ground.

                    ELENA
          Sorry, Inti. I understand that you
          don't believe me, I really do.

Inti calms down and takes a step towards Elena, putting a
hand on her shoulder as if to express that everything is
fine.

                    ELENA
          I just want to thank you once again
          for everything. For this
          opportunity, for trying to believe
          me, and for being my father.

                    INTI
          Mrs. Elena...

                    ELENA
          And I want to apologize to you.

                    INTI
          There's nothing to forgive,
          nothing...

PAF!

Elena interrupts Inti with a strong swipe of her cane. Inti
falls to the ground, half stunned. Elena yanks the watch off
him as Inti's nose begins to bleed and his stunned face of
surprise stares at her with wide eyes.

Elena walks away and lifts the watch, looking at Inti as if
asking for forgiveness for what she is about to do.

                    INTI
          No. Mrs. Elena... Don't you dare.

                    ELENA
          I'm sorry, Inti...

Crack!

Elena slams Inti's watch to the ground and finishes it off
with her cane. The watch is completely destroyed and left
lying on the ground.

                    INTI
          What is wrong with you, you crazy
          old hag?!

Inti looks behind the camera, as if looking for help.

                    INTI
          Is no one is going to do anything?

                    ELENA
          Dear Inti, you will now be able to
          witness your precious truth.

19 **INT. TIMELESS ROOM - DAY**   19

SUPERIMPOSED TEXT: Name: Pascual, Age: 16 years, Year: 1986.

On the same couch, there is a TEENAGER in a denim jacket with
patches, long hair and a skateboard. He has a cleft palate.

On the record player you can still listen to Mozart
(Divertimento in D Major).

                    TEENAGER
          I would go to the future. At least
          a hundred years in the future. I
          would see how things are: music,
          society, family... Even my
          grandchildren, maybe...

He thinks about it for a few seconds as he spins the wheels
of his skateboard.

                    TEENAGER
          I would see if we are finally
          treating animals in a dignified
          way... What cruelty they have had
          to go through because of human
          beings... At some point all that
          will end, I guess.

He keeps spinning the wheels of his skateboard.

                    TEENAGER
          I would also see if global warming
          was stopped or reversed in some
          way... Or if it didn't, maybe I
          could see the consequences of not
          reversing it and then return to the
          present to begin to change that
          catastrophic future... I don't
          know...

He looks behind the camera. They're giving him directions.

>   TEENAGER
>   Just once? Ah, I don't know...

Silence.

>   TEENAGER
>   I'd have to gamble for the future.
>   Despite everything that may happen,
>   there is something about the future
>   that reassures me. Going to the
>   past is more complex and also...,
>   if you travel too much to the
>   past..., how long can you withstand
>   without the comforts of the modern
>   world? No toilet paper, for
>   example.

20 **INT. TV SET, TALK-SHOW ATALAYA - NIGHT**   20

The first scene is repeated:

The deep, tired breathing of 90-year-old Elena can be heard in the darkness.

Between shadows and gloom, you can see on the floor: a table lamp that is flickering, as if about to explode and a bottle of red wine with a red label that is lying next to a broken glass that is still dripping, feeding a small pool of the same wine that looks like a pool of blood.

21 **INT. TIMELESS ROOM - DAY**   21

The schoolgirl stares at the camera.

22 **INT. TV SET, TALK-SHOW ATALAYA - NIGHT**   22

A small coffee table is lying around with a broken leg, a cheese and nut board is scattered all over the floor, and a fraction of a red neon sign with the letters "AT" colors the atmosphere.

23 **INT. TIMELESS ROOM - DAY**   23

The photographer from the 70's stares at the camera.

24 **INT. TV SET, TALK-SHOW ATALAYA - NIGHT** 24

   TV cue cards are scattered on the side of the table with the logo of the show "Atalaya" and a ball of green yarn is lying on the floor, half-disassembled, with no beginning or end.

25 **INT. TIMELESS ROOM - DAY** 25

   The woman from the future with an afro stares at the camera.

26 **INT. TV SET, TALK-SHOW ATALAYA - NIGHT** 26

   Elena's painted lips show traces of a cleft palate. She smiles and you can see some very white and well-kept teeth. Her blue eyes sparkle with excitement, behind huge golden optical lenses.

27 **INT. TIMELESS ROOM - DAY** 27

   The Elegant Huaso stares at the camera.

28 **INT. TV SET, TALK-SHOW ATALAYA - NIGHT** 28

   Elena is standing, leaning on her thin wooden cane. She takes a step forward, takes a couple of deep breaths, and calms down. She tucks her short hair behind her ears and shakes the dust off her long and elegant light gray cardigan, revealing her lavalier microphone.

                    ELENA
         Who would I be if at this point in
         my life, at this precise place in
         time, I wasn't willing to accept
         the risks I'm going to take?

29 **INT. TIMELESS ROOM - DAY** 29

   The burly painter from the 40's stares at the camera.

30 **INT. TV SET, TALK-SHOW ATALAYA - NIGHT** 30

   A little further back, on the floor and in pain, behind everything and near a fake wooden window showing a night city printed on paper, is INTI (35 years old), the host of the show, who seems to have been very well dressed up a few minutes ago. He rubs his face. His nose is broken, bleeding. He wears a large, light flannel shirt that also has his lavalier microphone hooked on.

31 **INT. TIMELESS ROOM - DAY** 31

The Groom from 2022 stares at the camera.

32 **INT. TV SET, TALK-SHOW ATALAYA - NIGHT** 32

Inti gets up little by little until he is standing. He grabs hold of an unlit spotlight, the kind that should be behind the camera to illuminate the set. He stands aloof, looking at Elena, perplexed.

Elena clears her throat. She stands firm and with a straight back. Now she is ready. She addresses the camera, the viewing audience, and speaks in a confident tone, as if it were a speech prepared for a long time.

>   ELENA
> My name is Elena Grajales and
> today, Monday, June 8th, 1998... I
> was lucky enough to be able to be
> here, with you.

Elena looks Inti in the eyes.

>   ELENA
> And for you, Inti, I will prove
> what we all thought impossible.

33 **INT. TIMELESS ROOM - DAY** 33

The lady in an apron from the 30's stares at the camera.

34 **INT. TV SET, TALK-SHOW ATALAYA - NIGHT** 34

Elena checks her analog wristwatch, one that is clearly very old and has a leather strap, with many details on it.

>   ELENA
> Without further ado, against all
> possible questioning, here and now,
> in front of all of you..., I, Elena
> Grajales, will travel back in
> time..., and I will accept all the
> consequences that this decision and
> this trip may cause.

A utter silence ensues. Inti just looks at her, expectant.

>   ELENA
> In 3... It's all worth it at this
> point.

Inti is going to say something, but he holds back. He approaches Elena slowly until she looks at him and he stops in his tracks. Elena stares at him until Inti decides to take a step back. Elena continues.

                    ELENA
        2... Because I finally know that
        this is what it should have always
        been.

35 INT. TIMELESS ROOM - DAY   35

The teen skateboarder from the 80's stares at the camera.

36 INT. TV SET, TALK-SHOW ATALAYA - NIGHT   36

Elena squeezes her cane firmly.

                    ELENA
           (whispering)
        Who would I be if I didn't do
        everything I could to be happy with
        my family?

Inti smiles and Elena smiles again. She stands tall and self-assured.

Elena looks at the camera, then at Inti and...

She presses the only button on her watch.

Inti takes a step further and gets closer to Elena.

Elena's eyes fill with emotion.

A deep sound begins to emerge and the lights begin to flicker. The sound gradually increases until:

BOOOOOOOOM!

A thunderous, high-pitched noise saturates the entire space.

                                        CUT TO BLACK.

37 INT. TIMELESS ROOM - DAY

Mozart's "Lacrimosa" is playing on the record player. Little by little and slowly brightening, all the characters that had previously appeared in the timeless room begin to appear: the schoolgirl, the photographer, the woman with an afro, the elegant huaso, the burly painter, the groom, the lady in an apron and the teenage skateboarder.

They all look at the camera without saying anything, as if they were posing for a photograph, in absolute silence, still, for long seconds.

Suddenly, the woman with an afro begins to sing "Lacrimosa," although her voice is not heard. Only the turntable version is heard.

                    WOMAN WITH AFRO
            Lacrimosa dies illa

The military politician joins the song. The woman with an Afro is still singing.

                    ELEGANT HUASO
            Qua resurget ex favilla

The skater from the 80's joins in.

                    ADOLESCENT
            Judicandus homo reus

The 9-year-old girl joins in.

                    SCHOOL GIRL
            Lacrimosa dies illa

The rest of the characters keep joining the singing one by one.

                    CORPULENT PAINTER
            Qua resurget ex favilla

                    PHOTOGRAPHER
            Judicandus homo reus

                    LADY WITH APRON
            Huic ergo parce, Deus

                    GROOM
            Pie Jesu Domine

They continue to sing together.

                        ALL
            Dona eis requiem
            Dona eis requiem
            Amen.

Once they finish, there is absolute silence and they are all
staring at the camera. We move on to a slow:

                                        FADE OUT.

                        THE END.

www.ingramcontent.com/pod-product-compliance
Lightning Source LLC
LaVergne TN
LVHW041615070526
838199LV00052B/3163